HUSBANDS, WIVES & WOLVES

Books by Fadhil Qaradaghi

Novels in Kurdish:

The Holy Boar (2006)
The Warlock of the Village (2007)
The Bigs and the Littles (2008, 2018)
(Under the title: *Come Back Home Our Beloved Stork*-2008)
A Murder in the Cretaceous Period (2018)

Nonfiction in Kurdish:

Ancient History of Kurdistan (5 Books)
Other Nonfiction in History, Religion, and Thought

Novels in English:
The Bigs and the Littles (2016)
A Murder in the Cretaceous Period (2017)
The Warlock of the Village (2018)
The Last Day of Sodom (2019)
The War of the Witches (2022)
The Last White Man (2023)
The Seventh Me (2023)

Fadhil Qaradaghi

HUSBANDS, WIVES
&
WOLVES

a novella

ZAGROS BOOKS

2024

Any resemblance between the rest of the names here and actual names is entirely coincidental. Some characters' names are inspired by the names of real people.

* * * * *

Image Credits:
1. Woman: Deane Bayas (pexels.com/@dbaler)
2. Man (edited): Giovanny Hernández Rodríguez (pexels.com/@giovanny-hernandez-rodriguez-117695757)
3. Wolf (edited): Bianca Van Dijk (pixabay.com/users/biancavandijk-9606149)

PART ONE

JAN BEFORE THE BITE

$$\mathbf{C\,h\,a\,p\,t\,e\,r \quad I}$$

Sweet Home

"Why?! Why?! Why?!"

Boom! Boom! Boom!

Both sounds came from Jan's bedroom.

"Stop it, Jan!" Vian, his wife, scolded him, calmly, though, while filing her nails.

"Mom! What's wrong with dad?" Tara, Jan's daughter, an eight-year-old, called out from her bedroom before coming into the living room.

Pink or dull red, Vian? her mother mused to herself, thinking of what color to use for her nails.

Dana, Tara's big brother, a fifteen-year-old boy joined his mother and sister in the room. He jumped onto the couch and bounced on it.

"Is it dad as usual?" he asked, still bouncing.

Jan shouted his unexplained protest again from the bedroom:

"Why?! Why?! Why?!"

Boom! Boom! Boom!

Always indifferent about his father harming himself, Dana answered himself, "Yes, it's him as usual. Dad's beating the wall with his head."

"Shut up, Dana!" the girl shouted at him, then asked her mother, "What's bothering my dad?"

"Ask him," Vian answered her, rotating her left hand's thumb to check the shine of the red under the light.

Boom! Boom! Boom!

The thud coming from both Jan's head and the wall continued. A spell of silence followed before he entered the living room, a line of blood running down his forehead between the nose and the right cheek.

Vian looked at him with her usual expression; half-shutting her eyes and a shadow of a scolding smile on her face.

"How are you going to answer your friends when they see this?" she asked him, her eyes still half-shut.

"How I'm going to answer my friends when they see your behavior?" Jan asked in turn.

The white, little, rotund, hairy dog moved toward Jan, sat on its legs, and barked at him. Jan gathered his lips for a strong, wrathful spit at the dog. His pain didn't let him do it.

"Get back, *shitlicker*," he shouted at the dog, instead.

The dog barked again.

Jan hated his daughter's dog. He hated it more when it barked at him. And it used to bark at him for trivial reasons, or even without a reason, as he had discovered lately.

His daughter asked, "Why were you beating the wall with your head, Dad?"

Dana asked, "Why was the wall beating your head, Tara's dad?"

"You shut up!" Jan told him.

Jan knew his son wouldn't be on his side. He was on the side of nobody except himself. Tara, on the other hand, used to abuse his fatherhood when she always treated him like a child and wanted him to play with her. Jan remembered he should let Tara have a share of his holy wrath with Dana.

"I mean you both shut up and forever. And also the third dog."

"Okay, Dad," Tara said. "Why were you beating the wall?"

"It was the wardrobe," Jan answered.

With full confidence, Tara said, "I know the sound of the wardrobe when your head beats it."

Dana added, "We know the sound of every piece of the house when you beat... I mean when they beat your head. And when it's a door, we know if it's the right or the left."

"And the two middle doors, Dad," Tara said.

"You know all that you know, but you don't know what you don't, eh?" Jan asked.

"Translate it, Mom," Dana said to his mother, his eyes still on his father.

Vian added a little touch to the last finger waiting in the queue.

"Ask your dad to translate it," she said.

"Forget it, you all," Jan said. "It was a one-moment memory loss."

"It doesn't matter," Tara said. "Now, you hurt yourself and you'll make it an *esxuse* to stop playing with me."

"Is this all that concerns you?" Jan asked. "Besides, it's excuse, buzzing mosquito."

"It's always who always bothers you," Dana said.

"Yes, it's always who…," Jan repeated, his voice trailing then. "What did you say? Translate it and stop barking at me."

"I didn't bark," Dana said.

"I mean Milo, the other dirty dog," Jan said, ending the sentence with a snarl.

Tara looked up at her father.

"Now, was it mom again?" the girl asked.

"Your mother; yes," Jan replied. "Your mother's unexplainable doings; yes and always."

Then cursing at no specific things or persons, he wiped the blood off his face with a tissue.

The dog barked again.

"Shut up your *shitful* mouth, Googy," Jan shouted at it.

"Don't talk to Milo, Jan," Vian said. "He hates your voice."

Similar to a whirlpool, the conversation continued this way. Jan and Vian were to Tara two immature and unreasonable adults. Dana ignored everything about all three and kept on his outings with his friends.

That morning, Vian invited her friends and their husbands for the day after tomorrow. Jan blamed her for not consulting him. She told him she didn't need to do as she could manage everything.

"How, by God, you'll manage to receive ten pairs of shoes at your door with only two days left?" he protested. "I didn't count the silly, retired Director General whom I expect to come wearing sandals and striped pajamas."

"Don't worry. I'll manage it," she answered, calm as always.

And the struggle began. But Jan was only complaining as he used to. He was just crying and protesting loudly. This was all he could do. Sometimes he butted a wall or a door. Other times when the situation was more drastic, or he thought it was so, he jumped on his chest on the floor and butted it.

This time, it was the turn of the wardrobe. Before reaching his destination, he heard his wife telling a friend of hers —the most talkative and consequently, gossiper number one in the squad— about his refusal to receive the guests.

Not waiting for his wife's second call, and believing it was now the drastic situation that needed a tougher object to butt, Jan shifted to the wall.

Vian was still chatting with her friend, now requesting that she inform the other guests, when Jan began a protest session of crying out and hitting his head against the wall.

Satisfied with the single call she made and considering it sufficient, Vian simply sat down and occupied herself with her nails.

That was the general situation before Jan entered the living room. For now, and still cursing, he wrapped his forehead with a white bandage. Dana waited until he finished.

"So, what was wrong this time, Dad?" Dana asked as if asking about the time.

Jan pointed at his face. "You're blind," he said. "You're always blind."

"I know it's mom's bothering stuff," Dana finally confessed. "Isn't it less harmful to beat her instead of beating your head?"

"Let him try it," his mother said calmly, then blew at the paint on her nail.

"One day I'll give it a shot," Jan replied, supposing he said it enthusiastically.

"You'll never do," Vian said.

"One day I'll give it a shot," Jan repeated, now less enthusiastically.

"No, darling," Vian said, again calmly and looking at her fingers. "You can only get angry and I'll climb the tree and everybody will see me there."

One day I'll give it a shot or something, he thought to himself, losing the last drop of enthusiasm.

Vian's threat was no surprise to him. His wife never acted normally. One day, he got angry with her —and it was one of his scarce violent reactions against her— and she went up the tallest tree in their garden. He had to beg her, after his fit of anger evaporated at a top speed, to come down, fearing that their neighbors and passersby would mock them.

Vian repeated this silent protest on two other occasions, and then Jan began to curse the tree every day. Eventually, he discovered that although cursing trees was easier than cutting them, the latter was more positive. To put his newfound philosophy into action, he bought an axe and started the job on the same day.

After the first axe, Vian went into the garden with half-shut eyes. And with a half, uninterested smile, she took the axe from him and went back inside without saying a word.

Their neighbor was watching from above the partition between the two houses. With his right forearm on the left and both on the wall and his chin on all —all to portray the typical view of a cold-blooded intruder— he attempted to ease his friend's embarrassment.

"Don't care about it," he told Jan.

"Care about what?" Jan asked, uneasy about the uninvited attempt.

"About what she did," his neighbor answered. "Women have strange behaviors. We, men, never can predict any of them."

No, Jan couldn't predict his wife's behaviors. He only experienced them; popping up mostly in the wrong place and time. At least, wrong to him. And again no, his neighbor's wife never acted weirdly — again, at least as much as he knew about their life.

Jan hated people offering advice about patience without themselves suffering and consequently practicing patience.

He hated every word said by his neighbor; a cold-blooded man with a round face and a bald head. He wished the man were hostile. Cold-blooded men were killing him, especially when they were rounded-faced and bald. And when clean-shaven, they looked like innocent babies whom Jan couldn't bear to harm.

But for that moment, he wished he hanged his neighbor on the tree. The man went inside, saving Jan from thinking of something he could do only in daydreams.

Instead of entertaining that imaginary possibility, Jan looked up at the treetop and said to himself:

Someone will be hanged or will hang himself or herself or itself or themselves on that strong branch above there. It'll be me or her or Milo the dog or the entire family. But in all probabilities, it won't be any of them except me.

Chapter 2

Leaving Sweet Home

Jan was in the living room, checking on the bandage around his head, when he noticed three travel bags, bulging as though filled with clothes. He turned around to find Vian.

"I owe her a dozen of thanks for not leaving when I was asleep," he said.

Vian came in.

"I'm going to pay my mom a visit," she told him.

"I guess you mean my mom," he said, himself not believing that was true. "She's only a few neighborhoods away from here and you don't need luggage. Unless, of course, you plan to spend a week with her."

He bit his lip, regretting he had brought up his mother. Whenever they visited her, she gave Vian a short lecture about good behavior. Vian's response was her usual facial expression: squinting and smiling. But now she would comment on her.

Strangely, she didn't.

"No, my mom," she explained.

To believe this was even more difficult. His mother-in-law resided in the UK. Vian had mentioned a journey across two continents to see her mother as if speaking about saying hello to a neighbor.

What about the tickets, for God's sake!? he said to himself in a loud inner voice ready to storm out his throat. *What about the visas!? Oh, shut up! We have still-valid visas. Okay. What about the tickets!?*

Vian exposed his thoughts, "You know we have six-month visas on our passports. And I purchased the tickets. For both of us."

That was one of the most characteristic things in her strange behavior. She decided in a second and acted in a fraction of a second. If Hell were walking on two feet in the neighborhood, she would've entered it after a quarter of a minute thinking —or even without thinking— to test it.

Jan felt his head becoming like a mushroom's cap. He thought of raising the white flag, though it was too early. But for Vian, it was late. Vian zipped a bag she left unzipped.

"Go change your clothes, darling," she said.

Jan gaped. This was even faster. Unable to close his mouth, he shut it with his thumb and index finger.

"No thanks, not with me," he said. "Go alone. I promise not to miss you even for a minute. I mean, I'll be thinking of you in everything I do as the song of the old lovely days said when I was a minus-nine-year-old potential newborn."

It was useless. It always was useless. He always refused, then protested (or protested and then refused). He discussed it again and protested more, sometimes whined and begged. And finally —if not submitting with more whining— he ended it by butting the wall or the door or the floor; which one was closer to him.

Jan looked at the wall next to him, then in the mirror. He touched the bandage on his forehead. It still hurt. He had a strong reason at the time to consider it dangerous to repeat yesterday's epic. He wished he could butt her head only one time in his life, but he needed an overdose of courage he never had. And also a great deal of hate against her, which he had none. Today, he had a greater excuse to not do it.

When my head gets well, I'll do it, he thought. *I swear to God I'll do it.*

And he knew he lied. But he had an excuse, anyway, and this relieved him. Even without any excuse, he wouldn't have done it. He loved her. It was that simple. But she hurt him. It was that simpler.

He was used to vowing to do this or that thing against his wife, but he could put none into action. As a consequence of breaking his oaths, he had to pay food or money for the poor as the religious instructions ordered in such cases; food for ten poor people for each broken oath. And because the cases were as many as the days of the year, he had to pay a lot of money.

On the contrary, if he vowed to do something for Vian, the religious instructions didn't allow him to break his oath and he had to do the thing for her and pay more than the food for ten people. For both cases, Jan had a fixed item in his budget.

So, now he had to add the new amount of money to the already-inflated oath-breaking account.

He wanted to ask her about her decision and say: "Why so abruptly?" But it was silly to question things mixed with her blood. One should ask her: "Why not abruptly?"

Any day she hesitated to do something, it meant there was something wrong with that thing, not with her.

It took the spouses only two hours to be ready for departure and say the last goodbye to the surprised daughter and the indifferent son and the clueless nanny who had just started her temporary job. The taxi driver bowed to pick up the last bag when Vian jumped into the passenger seat. The driver stopped halfway and stayed bowing. Jan grinned.

"My wife suffers from motion sickness, especially when in the backseat," he explained to the driver. "She even may throw up."

"Ah, yes," the driver said, picking up the bag. He threw it in the trunk while still looking at Vian.

"Don't be afraid," Jan told him. "As long as she's in the passenger seat, she won't vomit."

"I think I understand you," the driver said without explaining what he understood.

The cab had moved only a few minutes when Vian abruptly said, "Go downtown. I want to take a look at it before I leave."

The driver gaped. He kept looking ahead.

"I think I'm going to make an accident," he said.

"We'll be late, Vian," Jan said.

"We've got plenty of time," she said.

"It'll cost you much, madam," the driver said.

"We'll be late, Vian," Jan repeated.

"It's a long drive, madam," the driver explained.

"Not your business. Just go," Vian said, not angry, but smiling.

It was time for Jan's white flag. He repeatedly poked the driver on the shoulder.

"Don't argue. Just go. Just go," he said to him.

The man looked over his shoulder, gaping again. Then he shrugged.

"I'm the idiot among these three," he said. "They'll pay me, so why should I discuss it? You'll pay me, madam. Won't you?"

Vian moved her thumb back.

"He'll pay," she said, looking at the city.

The driver turned to Jan again.

"Since you'll be the one who'll pay, do you want me to make sharp turns?"

"In case you want her to throw up right on your lap," Jan answered.

"Ah, I understand. May God help you, my friend," the man said. "And you'll go all that way, that manner, that abrupt behavior, abroad? Where to? If not a national security secret."

"The UK," Vian answered, instead.

The man whistled in amazement.

"The UK!" he exclaimed.

"On an airplane," Jan said, "if you are curious about national security secrets."

"I see," the man said. "As much as I know from movies, the windows of the planes aren't openable."

"And unbreakable except in movies," Jan said. "So, in real life, someone can't throw another someone out."

He turned to look at the city, feeling that he needed to lash himself.

Don't ever think of something you can never do, idiot husband, Jan thought to himself. *Even if it's a movie, you won't do it and will ask the filmmaker to change the scene to let you, yourself, jump. Idiot! Idiot!*

C h a p t e r 3

The Sorrows of Adult Jan

Jan was ready for every unpleasant surprise. Nevertheless, he longed for a surprise like a sudden boom of a thousand guns; a drastic thing Vian would do and would end up canceling the journey. But with bad luck embracing Jan like a passionate lover, his wife was at her top condition of normal manner.

Pulling a roller bag, Jan followed Vian like an obedient child. That wasn't the case in their first travel when he liked the journey but she was nervous even before going into the airport area. In fact, it wasn't their first time on board because it didn't even start because Vian canceled it. Since then, each traveled alone. Jan believed that spouses traveling alone was the greatest invention in history.

Like a clever little girl pupil standing before a serious teacher, Vian stood before the officer who looked at their passports. Jan guessed she behaved herself on purpose, which was to make a successful journey. The officer looked at Jan's forehead.

"You must've hurt yourself very recently, sir," the officer said.

Jan opened his mouth to answer. Vian was faster.

"Of course, he has hurt himself," she said. "Unless you think he hides drugs under the bandage."

As Jan was interrupted, he was supposed to shut his open mouth. But he didn't. Gaping, he received the officer's stare of suspicion.

"Will you please untie your bandage," the officer uttered the demand Jan expected.

"Of course not," Jan answered with a half-open mouth. "I mean I'm afraid the injury would bleed."

"Worry nothing. We have a doctor here to help you," the officer said, taking Jan's arm with his hand to both go somewhere.

Guessing it to be the clinic, he submitted without useless objection. On his way with the officer, Jan looked over his shoulder to see if Vian was shocked. She wasn't.

"They won't hold you up, my dear," she said to him.

As she expected, Jan returned a few minutes later. His eyes were half-shut with the pain he suffered when untying the bandage and then tying it again. The officer was still taking him by the arm; this time to help him walk on his feet.

"I'm sorry, sir," the officer said. "And you, madam, be more careful about your words here and at every airport. Injuries and drugs can be checked in minutes. Some other words can keep you detained under interrogation for hours and maybe days."

"Words like 'terrorists' or 'bombs'?" Vian asked, smiling.

The officer shut his eyes and lifted his head to the ceiling. "My God!" he said.

Jan grabbed Vian by the arm. "Let's go. It's late. Thank you, sir, for everything," he said, nearly panting.

With his hand pulling her, he hurried to the check-in counter. Vian was resisting and leaning backward.

"What did they ask you about?" she inquired of him.

"Nothing serious," he answered. "Only about you. I mean if you were… sorry, if you were sane."

"I am sane," she said.

"No, you are not," he said between his teeth.

"What did you say?"

"I said if you don't want this journey to see the light of the next dawn, let's go back before we finish it in detention," he answered.

Vian said nothing.

They put the bags on the conveyor belt. Jan saw Vian's eyes following them and read a bad intention in them. He got ready to jump and roll his arms around her to stop her; in case. She stayed unmoving.

Jan kept her eyes on her until they got on the plane.

"Like the movies, the real disaster is going to take place now," he whispered to himself.

And he was right.

Vian awkwardly threw her carry-on over the overhead bin, then threw herself onto the window seat. She stayed a while before she asked Jan to change seats. Then she stood up and kept standing when the flight attendant ordered the passengers to buckle their seatbelts.

"I think you heard me, madam," the woman told Vian. "Please take your seat and fasten your seatbelt."

"I feel comfortable," Vian said, looking at nowhere.

Jan saw the attendant's smile of irritation. She said nothing for a while, then turned and walked to the back of the airplane.

"Now, she'll bring the security men with her," Jan told his wife without daring to look back.

"So what?" she said, glancing sideways to detect the return of the attendant.

"So, they'll arrest you, or at best kick you out."

Vian's eyes showed the scarce moments of hesitation when unable to decide on going on her stubbornness.

She'll submit this time, Jan thought. *I'm sure.*

And she did.

When the flight attendant returned with a security man, Vian had sat with the seatbelt around her waist. Pretending to be happy, she was smiling and looking through the window at the blank space outside. The security man looked at the attendant.

"It seems to be a hard flight," he told her.

"If there'll be any flight at all," she commented.

The man asked her what to do. She shrugged and walked to the cockpit. Moving back to his seat, the man looked over his shoulder at Vian who answered him with a broad smile and waggling her right fingers hello to him.

Vian's broad smile was still on her face when she turned to Jan.

"I'll like this flight," she said. "What about you?"

"If this flight won't kill us, then we'll live for a thousand years," he answered.

She turned ahead, still smiling. "Oh, dear Mom. I wonder how much you'll be delighted to see me knocking on your door," she said as if singing a song.

"In the UK, they ring the bells like we do," Jan said, thinking that making a joke would keep Vian's ocean waveless.

Vian turned again to him. "In poetic language, they use 'knock on the door' even if there's a bell's button on the wall," she said. "By the way, please, don't butt her doors whatever happens."

"Isn't her house insured?" he asked, then touched his bandaged forehead. "No butting any door before one month according to the doctor's prescriptions," he said. "And ringing the bell is as romantic as knocking on the door."

When the plane began to taxi out on the runway, Vian let out a low cry of joy. To Jan's luck, only the close neighbors heard the cry, and none reacted.

"If everything goes like this," Jan told himself, "our journey will end with zero losses."

The first half of the journey proved to him that he had built his optimistic expectations on a false premise. He had to endure successive miseries:

First, Vian going frequently to the lavatory without needing it; only to take a walk, as she told him. Jan's protest that the passengers were watching her was of no use. Then, needless cries at mild clear-air turbulence and when the others only hissed and sighed. And finally, her trying to give a lecture to the passengers about how to behave in foreign countries and that quickly turned into a medley of short topics.

The flight attendant heard her at the fifth topic and ordered her, as firmly as she could, to shut up. Knowing he could do nothing and embarrassed to death, Jan took out a book from his little bag and pretended to be absorbed in reading, all the while sneaking sidelong glances at his wife. When the flight attendant finished scolding his wife, she reached out and turned his upside-down book right side up, handing it back to him.

Jan looked up at the attendant and read her eyes saying, "I understand you, poor fellow."

But this also Jan handled upside down.

Keep your eyes on your mad wife, stupid man, she had said to herself, in fact.

The second half of the journey was disastrous in the exact meaning of the word.

Vian suddenly jerked in her seat and shouted, "Give me the vomit bag. Give it to me quickly."

All passengers turned to her. The flight attendant hurried to check the new problem. Jan's eyes rolled. He was sure it was another game. Vian bowed and pressed her forehead on the back of the seat before her. The flight attendant rested a hand on her back and leaned forward.

"The bag's a few centimeters before you, madam," she told Vian.

Vian didn't respond. The attendant took the bag and gave it to her. Vian retched. The attendant's trained ears didn't miss the fake vomiting. To give herself an opportunity for another rebuke, the attendant gently took the bag from Vian, looked inside it, and smiled.

"What does this mean?" she asked Vian.

With her forehead on the seat before her, Vian turned her face to the young woman.

"The period came to me," she whispered. "It hurts like tens of knives in my belly. I couldn't say it before the passengers."

She shook her head quickly up and down and gave the attendant a smile of pain.

Jan was hearing and praying.

Only God knows how this will end, he thought.

"How old are you?" the attendant asked Vian.

"Thirty-eight," Vian answered.

Jan heard only "thirty." He guessed the other to be "one."

In such circumstances, Vian never could say little lies, he thought, then he pondered over the sentence he said to understand it. It looked just nonsense.

Despite her wish to feel sympathy for Vian, the attendant didn't wish to believe her. But she couldn't say it, either. There was no legal way to check the truth. Vian won this time, the attendant admitted to herself. And to hide her embarrassment in case Vian had deceived her, she straightened and patted her on the shoulder.

"You'll feel better," she said loudly enough to let the neighbors hear. "I can bring you anti-vomiting pills if you'd like, although it's getting late. Those pills should usually be taken before boarding the plane."

Vian understood her suspicions.

"I'll be fine," she said, loudly likewise, and painfully. Then she added with a triumphant voice, slightly twisting her trunk, "Thaaaank yoooo."

The attendant's eyes narrowed and her lips pursed with a smile of challenge.

"You're welcome," she said. Then she said to herself, *You won't get away with it that easily the next time, noisy kid.*

C h a p t e r **4**

The Sorrows of Adult Jan

Continued

Half an hour later, Vian was watching a movie and laughing. It bothered Jan who saw nothing funny in the movie. Nevertheless, he kept his comments to himself since Vian was laughing to herself. Despite hating her reasonless laughter, he wished the movie lasted forever. And as if Vian was watching his thoughts, she shut off the screen, stood up, and began to take a video with her cell phone. She recorded the cockpit first, then slowly rotated 180 degrees. Jan tucked down her jacket.

"It's forbidden," he hissed with a dry throat.

"No, it's not," Vian said, smiling and continuing filming.

The flight attendant came out from the cockpit. She halted on seeing Vian.

"Here we go again," she said.

Ready to lose her job, she approached Vian with a rigid posture.

"Somebody pushed the call light," the attendant said, loudly. "Who's complaining?"

A woman lifted a hand and then pointed at Vian who kept recording as if nothing had to do anything with her.

"Stop recording, madam," the attendant ordered her. "It's forbidden."

"It isn't," Vian said, zooming her cell phone in and out on aged spouses. "I know the rules."

"No, you don't," the attendant said, covering the camera with a hand. "It's prohibited to record the passengers without their consent. And when they complain, it's definitely prohibited."

Vian turned the cell phone away from the young woman's hand to record another side of the plane. Jan was slipping down in his seat until he sunk in it. There was no place to hide. Not even under the seat in front of him.

Fed up with the unruly passenger, the attendant tried to take the phone from her. Vian jerked.

"You don't have the right to take it," she protested.

"Yes, I have. I also have the right to restrain you," the woman said.

"No, I won't let you."

The woman rolled her arms around Vian.

"Give it to me," she shouted.

Jan sunk more in his seat.

"Let go of me," Vian shouted in turn.

Suddenly, the attendant forgot her job and acted as any other woman would do in such a situation. She tugged Vian's hair. Vian's head tilted, but she didn't try to free her hair. She continued recording the passengers. The woman beat the cell phone with the other hand. Vian tried to bend down to pick up the phone.

"No, you won't," the woman raged, then began a brawl with Vian, who surprisingly —for the passengers but not for Jan— didn't fight back. She only protested. And to make the attendant more puzzled, Vian protested calmly.

The passengers showed indifference, but in fact, they enjoyed watching the scene. A man commented with a merry voice that women-fight, especially when they tugged each other's hair, was the most enjoyable fighting scene.

Jan had consumed the last inch of the available space of his seat to sink when the security men and the crew interfered to stop the fight. They tried in vain to force Vian to sit down on her seat. And as the plane was flying on the ocean, the crew used the last resort. They taped Vian to her seat. Vian protested a little louder than before. They were about to gag her when she submitted.

"No, no!" she shouted. "I'll keep quiet."

The crew shared glances. Then all turned to the flight attendant who shook her head unbelieving. The crew interpreted her gesture as consent to not gag the noisy passenger. Satisfied with taping Vian, the attendant didn't rectify it for them. She turned to the troublemaker with her forefinger on her lips.

"Hush or we will hush you," she told Vian.

To the surprise of everyone, Vian responded with quick nods and a broad smile.

The attendant couldn't believe that the annoying woman had submitted like this. She judged that Vian would not stick to her promise for a long time surrounded by plastic tape.

The crew left for the cockpit. Vian, again surprisingly — this time even for Jan— began to sing a calm, joyful song.

Pondering over this last behavior that he never experienced made Jan forget to straighten in his seat. He made his calculations and analysis in his sunken posture.

"Sit back in your seat, my dear," Vian told him as gently as she could.

"Not before you explain it to me," he said from below.

"Explain what, darling?"

"You, refusing to fight, and you begging them not to gag you."

"Why should I fight? I got what I wanted."

Jan jolted upright, now back in his seat.

"How many passengers are on this plane?" he asked.

"Not fewer than two hundred," Vian answered.

"One hundred ninety-nine people here are smart while number two hundred is a fool," he said. "And the fool is I who love to waste my time."

"You won't lose anything if you waste your time with your wife," she said.

But this wasn't what Jan meant. Vian's answer turned his analysis of her character upside down.

First, he thought she felt comfortable when people treated her with violence. Her answer put a cross on this and told him she loved to do everything she loved to do despite the consequences. And nothing was new in this. As such, she was Vian whom he used to know.

He began an inner dialogue:

Two hundred passengers are a small number of people. The only idiot on this Earth is me. I still can't understand her. Oh, if only it was the former.

What former, idiot?

Don't you understand, you foolish? I mean if it was that she loves to be treated with violence.

Yes, dear idiot, if only it was this, I would've beaten her every day. At least once a day and twice on vacations.

Right, foolish, and three times in the Eid.

He looked at her, seeing her still singing with joy.

Of course, in case I got the courage to do it.

Which he hadn't.

Or if I get to hate her.

Which he didn't believe he could do.

So, no beating. No violence. Okay with whining and complaining. The greatest goal should be safety. And safety with Vian came through zero problems, zero activities, zero talking.

This was Jan's significant conclusion. But again, nothing was new. The whirlpool brought him to the start point. And the place was an airplane. He didn't want the crew to tape him, otherwise, he would have butted the window with his injured head.

Unexpectedly, he fell asleep. He saw a mash-up of dreams with Vian's song in the background. He once chased her. Then she chased him all the time. She was giggling and he was whimpering. Finally, he jumped on his chest on the floor of the airplane and began to beat it with his forehand and cry. Vian approached him, bounding. She opened her mouth to its full extent and showed sharp teeth while he was still harming himself and crying. Vian bent over and bit his butt. Jan opened his mouth with pain to shout a holler. But suddenly he gritted his teeth, narrowed his eyes with anger, snarled, circled his lips, and howled like a wolf: "Awoooo!"

And he opened his eyes wide.

Vian turned to him. He stayed a while staring ahead to examine the reality of being awake.

"Were you dreaming, my dear?" Vian asked him.

Jan turned and saw whom he guessed to be the pilot. He thought the man had come to check on him, but before wasting words thanking him, he saw him talking to his wife. The pilot was crouching beside Vian's seat and placing a hand on its handle. He looked as if bargaining with her.

Jan heard Vian answering a question from the pilot he missed.

"Let me think of it," she said.

"Quickly, please," the pilot urged her.

Vian turned to her husband.

"What would you say, darling?" she asked him.

"Anything rids us from this damn plane," Jan answered.

Vian turned back to the pilot.

"It's a deal," she told him.

"A deal for what?" Jan asked.

"This gentleman offers not to submit me to the police in the airport in exchange for accepting the apology of the woman who beat me."

"It's not called apology," Jan yelled. "It's called 'not to sue the woman who beat you'."

The pilot frowned on hearing the word "suing."

"Does this make any difference?" Vian asked him, innocently.

"Yes, it does," Jan yelled again, this time enthusiastically. "Suing means compensation and a great deal of money."

"Who will pay who?" she asked.

"They'll pay you, Lulu," he answered. "You'll force them to pay you."

And immediately he bit his lip. He had forgotten number one in his wife's characteristics: anything he suggested she refused at once, and without thinking about it. He turned to the window. With all his heart, he wished to beat it with his injured head —or, smash his head with it, or smash both.

"No, my dear. An apology is enough," Vian's reply came, quick and simple.

Jan was still turning to the window. He rocked in his place, theoretically practicing his last reaction to his wife's behavior: butting the nearest object to him.

"It's a deal, madam," the pilot said. "Will you please join us in the cockpit to make the settlement?"

She stood up with a broad smile and preceded the pilot. Jan heard the comments of the passengers. And unlike in most cases where opinions vary, the comments about him were almost unanimous, like a common consensus:

"They cheated your wife, poor man," one man said.

"He knows that," another in the next back seat said.

Thank you, Mister, Jan thought to himself.

But the mister had something else to add.

"But he's too weak to convince her."

I withdraw it, Jan thought.

"She deserves it," the first man's wife said. "She bothered us through the entire journey."

"No, he deserves it," the second man said. "He's nothing but a big loser."

"I bet his wife has beaten him on the forehead," said the old woman whom Vian had filmed with her husband.

"I agree," her old husband said. "He seems to be a coward."

"What do you want to say?" a young woman in front of him said while turning to him. "He's a coward because he doesn't beat his wife?"

"No. Because she beats him," the old man said.

"It's the same thing," the woman said.

"No, it isn't," the old man said. "It's an irreversible equation. I'm a retired math teacher and I know scientific facts well. The absolute fact in this case is that he's a chicken. Do you agree?"

"Yes, I agree that he's a chicken," she said. "And everyone here agrees. Do you all agree?"

The passengers yelled, "Oh, yeah, yeah, we all agree."

"And he's a big loser," yelled the man whom Jan misunderstood.

"Don't be rude to him," a middle-aged woman said. "He's only an idiot."

You're wrong, madam, Jan thought. *I'm both: an idiot and a chicken. I won't relinquish either.*

Comments kept beating Jan like this. Only his eyes moved; one time to the right when the speakers were on his right, and the other more to the right when they were behind, and then ahead, and so on. Nobody gave him the right to defend himself. He knew it was all because of his wife bothering them, and he had to pay the price.

Vian came back, smiling and proud of herself. She took her seat.

"Not everyone has the opportunity to go into the cockpit and see all that stuff and those wonderful guys," she said, pushing her hair back from her left ear

Jan opened his mouth to say something —anything as he couldn't know what to exactly say. The voice from the cockpit didn't allow him. Amid the low clamor of the passengers, the captain requested them to get ready for touchdown. The word "down" inspired Jan to say the thing he didn't know to say.

"Did you note down anything to them?" he asked.

"Yes, I did," she answered. "Were you spying on us?"

"Now, any footage any passenger took won't be of any use," he said. "If you didn't sign their papers, you would've used the footage as evidence and gained a lot of money as compensation."

"You don't know how they respected me," she said, still smiling. "The pilot asked me to take his seat. Oh, how lovely that was. Only one out of one million people can get such an opportunity."

"You could've got one million dollars, Lulu."

"Oh, stop it," she said, closing her eyes and lifting her head.

If it was Milo, the dog, she would've accepted its suggestion, but it was mine, he thought. *Forget it dumb Jan and get ready for the catastrophes of the rest of your journey. And there'll be dozens of them. Stupid Jan! Stupid and chicken like all the passengers agreed to call you.*

Chapter 5

In the Great City

The warm hugs and kisses Rangeen, Jan's mother-in-law, and her daughter exchanged at Gatwick Airport didn't mean to him that everything would go smoothly with the two women. It was only in his first year with Vian when he got the lovely illusion that women kissing each other would mean a peaceful life.

When the two women finished, Jan gained one short hello. It was more than he demanded as it meant to him as much as turning on the light after midnight to go to the restroom would mean to ordinary people.

The scene of the warm reception made Jan not think of any expected disastrous short journey from the airport to Rangeen's house; a ride that would be nothing compared to a flight. Taking a seat in a car was less dangerous than flying although there was a guaranteed chance of jumping out of a car but not out of an airplane.

Rangeen and her daughter chattered all the way to the old woman's house. This made it a noisy ride but completely safe, except for Vian now and then expressing annoying excitement.

Vian interrupted the chatter several times with uncontrolled reactions at seeing the city that she had seen before. She poked her head out of the passenger window and waved her hand to the uninterested people who were —by chance or by a merciful plan of Fate, Jan judged— White cold-blooded and old-fashioned English. Rangeen kept telling her daughter to bring back her intruder head in and roll up the window.

All three of them entered Rangeen's flat, where another wave of hugs and kisses followed. Finally, Jan got the second hello, which he counted as an extravagance in the wrong place for the wrong person.

From that point on, Jan received little attention while the two women continued chattering until a late hour of the night.

At least, I won't need violent protests, he thought to himself in his bed while feeling at his bandaged forehead.

Only then, did he wonder why his mother-in-law didn't ask her daughter about the damage that presumably he — not she— made to his body.

"Did she know that her daughter stood behind it and she saved her some unnecessary questions and answers?" he asked himself and immediately fell asleep before he could answer himself.

The first activity the next afternoon was the expected mundane pilgrimage to the markets. To Jan's luck, the two women didn't need a man with them, especially the kind of man he was. At least not for now since it was too early to need a porter. Yet, he joined them.

Jan spent his time idly in what most men thought to be the foulest time in the dirtiest task; shopping. Those men's share was to sit in the café, having hot drinks and thinking of nothing and then having cold drinks and again thinking of nothing, and finally wondering if they should have hot or cold drinks.

Waitresses were going here and there. They gave him the opportunity to ponder over philosophical topics. He wondered why businessmen always chose women. It was to attract men, he guessed. It was to bring more customers. But male waiters attracted women, too. No. He rebutted it. Only men's personality and tidiness attracted women. Male waiters had nothing of both. They were just waiters in the uniform. This was inhumane and unfair. Male waiters were also human beings. It pleased Jan to blame women at this point.

On the other hand, women attracted men whether in the uniform or even without —and especially without— anything on them.

He looked around to see if anybody was nearby and reading his thoughts. He or she would accuse him of one of the pre-cooked, or as he liked to describe it, using engineering terms: pre-cast, labels. And there were many of them ready: you are biased, sexiest, retarded, uncivilized, recently graduated from a cafe, a monkey escaping from a forest, or any other term the modern civilization had invented or would invent.

Sometimes calamities were so grieving they brought laughter —he suddenly remembered this fact. He chuckled. Then he laughed at his misery. Whether a man or a woman, they would judge him for something, whatever it would be. Then he smiled.

"Why not fight the world since the world was fighting me?" he asked himself.

The question gave him a moment of bravery and self-confidence. But it was just one moment.

His wife was more beautiful than most of the waitresses. A good topic to change the gloomy topics. But he never thought of her beauty or saw it. At least after the first year of their marriage. He was harming his body and she was harming her charm.

And it was time for pre-cast steel-reinforced solutions. A solution in a book. Authors loved to give magical solutions.

In books, of course, Jan thought.

"Like the golden title: 'Pay only ten dollars for my book and become a millionaire'," he said. "Thousands will buy the book but then only the author becomes a millionaire."

Fortune was the last thing he thought of. He needed only one thing: manhood.

His phone displayed an ad for a book:

HOW TO BE A REAL MAN.

"Bah! When you finish this book you'll change into a real man as long as you don't forget to say abracadabra every time you wet your thump and flip a page," he said.

Another book:

MANHOOD.

"Easier than acquiring manhood is to become Rubin Hood holding a bow with a helicopter chasing you from among skyscrapers."

The third:

BE A MAN.

"It's more like a swear word than a book title. No, thanks."

The fourth was more reasonable:

HUSBANDS' DIPLOMATIC SUCCESS.

"Judging on the book title, it's an 'Open Sesame' formula. Judging from the book description, it's a bootlicking success. If you don't gain success after reading this book, you'll at least master shining your wife's boots using your tongue."

Every title in the list was promising. None was convincing.

"Isn't there any book like 'How to Beat Your Wife and Escape the Problem With Minimum Losses'?"

There wasn't any and he didn't need any because he never thought of beating Vian. In fact, he had thought of it, but he couldn't. Even if he could, he didn't want to.

"Oh, no. I'm saying this fact again and again," he said, wishing he could shout it.

And he never hated her. No. He even loved her. But she made him suffer. This was the simplest description for the hardest problem.

The waitresses were smiling at him. It was an invitation. Not for love, but to eat and drink more and spend more.

Every smile would cost him some extra pounds for the stuff he would order. Even the VAT was calculated in those calculated emotions, and so the smiles were broader by one percent point something.

In business, emotions were weighable and payable; exactly like groceries. But there was no way to deal with that problem. Accept it or refuse it. It would pop up before you here and there, whether now or later. Besides, many people —or most of them, who can tell?— didn't consider it a problem at all.

Finally, he bought a book from the little shop opposite him: How To Deal With Your Stubborn Wife.

The woman cashier raised her eyebrows. Jan smiled like a child.

"It's for my friend," he explained. "A friend and a neighbor and a third-degree man although he's bald." Then he smiled again, running his fingers into his hair to prove that the book wasn't for him.

"Modern researches proved that the more bald the more having manhood," he added. "But my neighbor is unlucky because he's the exception in the rule."

The young woman smiled in return.

"All of us seek such advice for our friends," she said.

Jan thought it was a cheeky comment because it meant, "And all of us are lying because it's for us, not for our friends."

Jan gave her his credit card. Curious to know the name of the stranger, she read it.

"Thank you, Yan," she said.

Jan looked over his shoulder.

"Answer her, Yan," he said to the air behind him.

"Isn't this your name?" she asked.

"Yan?" he asked. "I thought you meant a German guy behind me. Do I look like a German?"

"Maybe Danish or Dutch," she said.

"All makes no difference," Jan said. "All are the same to me. The same old blue-eyed imperialists."

"Or a wrong spelled French?"

"Why are you insisting on European nationalities?" Jan asked. "Couldn't be Indian?"

A female voice from behind reminded him that he was practicing his typical characteristic: prolonging a discussion that he could end with one straightforward answer.

Vian had finished her joined job with her mother. It was time for the last job in the operation which the man in the group must have done; the weigh-less and wage-less porter.

I'll do everything for you, Lulu, but please don't perform your usual embarrassing shows, he thought.

And for his good luck, Vian did none. Jan got out with it without loss, except for the few pounds he paid for the book.

"Which I'll use its papers to clean the bottom of my shoes with," he said.

C h a p t e r **6**

Dreams and Reality

Things went at a slow routine in the Old City. It would have been boring for Jan in other locations and times as nothing odd was happening. On the contrary, he enjoyed the days with the nothing-happening circle. But finally, things should have happened which were the unpleasant incidents he feared. The difference was that it was Vian's mother, not him, who had to face them. Jan felt like a grace that he had become a footnote at the mouse-eaten bottom of a water-washed page. Only a single incident directly touched him, and it only bothered his tranquil mood, letting him emerge from it unscathed.

The day before heading back home, Vian read an announcement for a modern art exhibition in a newspaper advertisement that she had torn out. Only the place and the date were intact. Vian's mother tried in vain to steer her away from that peculiar intention. It was eleven pm and no exhibition in any place on any planet in the universe would be open at such an hour, she told her daughter, intending to implore her rather than provide facts and information.

Jan, too, presented his arguments —echoes; moreover, weak echoes of those his mother-in-law said, but intended to provide concrete facts without trying to implore his wife.

Let them both go to the Midnight Inferno exhibition, he thought, *and let the Iron Boss share my daily hemlock juice.*

Jan used to call the old woman "The Iron Boss." Vian's bullheadedness, on the other hand, was something else: stiffer than iron and more unpredictable than kids' whims. And she wrapped all that in the calmness that was at odds with how stubborn people usually appeared and acted.

"I can't join you in this crazy outing," Jan said to Vian, not serious about calling it craziness.

He was glad he had said something different from his mother-in-law's words. Vian aborted his delight in less than five seconds.

"Who asked you to join us?"

Jan felt his nose throbbing and turning red, and then throbbing more and becoming redder. A clout in the face at 11 pm. Hospitals were shut. Ambulance drivers were asleep, drunk, or dead. Homeless went home.

Jan looked at his mother-in-law like a rabbit. He saw the Iron Boss replying to his glance with a face 70% bewildered, 10% embarrassed, and 10% undefinable feeling.

Even if hundred percent ashamed, he thought, *she's her daughter and she'll cover for her. But no one will give the dog a hand.*

One month later, Jan knew that the woman was struggling to suppress her anger and save her dignity before the bandaged, red-nosed dog when she said in a low voice coming out from clenched teeth and resembling the tires braking on a pebbles road, "Okkkayyy, let's gooo."

The Boss turned to him. "You're welcome to come and see," she said.

To see what, my MIL? The shut-doors exhibition for pre-bed era art, or to see your daughter kicking the door and breaking the windows?

Silently, the skull-on-knee group went out, and then got into the car, again silently. Jan's mother-in-law turned on the engine in the silence of the outside world in a sudden way that caused Jan to jerk in his backseat. The two women didn't notice him. Each was absorbed in her world. Jan, too, was absorbed in his world and had no right but to protest and whimper and jerk.

Rangeen drove straightforwardly for a while, then turned right twice. One right U-Turn. It was like a circle. Then a byway.

Will you turn left, please? Just for change. Thanks.

Another byway. A two-way street. And here the exhibition was on the other side of the street; shut and dark except for one inside white, cold light showing a hall from the windows, void of anyone. Vian half shut her eyes with sorrow.

Rangeen turned to her while keeping the car going to its destination.

"What did you expect?" she asked. "To be crowded with lunatics like…?"

Yes, say it, dear MIL, Jan thought. *Like the idiot in the backseat.*

"You see you brought us for nothing," Rangeen went on.

So, it wasn't me, Jan said to himself. *But maybe she forgot there's a dog in the backseat. If I'm wrong and she knew about the dog, then there's progress in evaluating her daughter.*

"I wanted to take photos," Vian said, turning over her shoulder to Jan. "Maybe another time."

"There'll be no another time," the dog barked from the backseat. "We're leaving tomorrow."

"Are you still there?" his mother-in-law asked.

"Arf!" the dog answered with a short, mute bark. Then loudly, "Yelp!"

The short journey ended the way it started: silently. And then all went to bed, always silently. Only Jan got out of it with a victory. Yet, the two women didn't allow him to celebrate it by letting him see them arguing.

Jan sat in the bed with a smile of contentment on his face, and then slowly reclined. The phantom of a triumphant leader soared in the sky of the room. He remembered he was in London.

"How about Churchill who overcame the German giant with lots of tears and blood and more bombs on German cities?"

But many things spoiled the memory.

"Do you choose one with a high hat and a cigar in one corner of the mouth and a face like a sprouting potato? And celebrating in an old-fashioned, funny car? What about losing the elections after his victory? No. No. Long live the ancient emperors! Down with the English potato!"

Rome was the other great city that invaded the world. He liked it more:

A Roman emperor rolling his arm around his helmet and surrounded by officers and soldiers, all heading for the gates of Rome. On Capitol Hill and before the temple of Jan-Jupiter; boyfriend of Vian-Venus (her temple recently shut off for repairs), the senate body was waiting for him with a purple toga and a laurel wreath. The citizens were cheering. The music was loud and noisy. The city garrison was hollering their leader's triumph. Mangonels were hurling primitive fireworks. Pagan lions were feasting on Christian believers.

Jan submitted to the scenario and waited for sleep to come to continue it and show Vian among the audience, biting her fingers with sorrow and remorse.

He fell asleep and the dream was ready:

He was alone in a fog-covered plain. Dogs barked from afar. Their savage barking grew louder as they approached. They leaped toward him. Crying with horror, he ran away and they chased him. Frightened and wailing, he looked at his hands leaping before him. He, too, was a dog.

One dog caught up with him and he cried like a child. The dog bit him. He let out a long cry of pain and fell on his face. Vian came with the stick of a broom to beat him. She raised the stick, and one moment before she moved it down, he jerked up, now strong and angry. He had turned into a shaggy wolf, frowning with eyes sparking fire. He ran toward a cliff, jumped on its top in one leap, and with the full moon in the background, he stood ready for the next dramatic scene.

Jan the wolf lifted his head, looked at the moon, and howled, "Awooooo."

All the wolves in the plains and valleys echoed his call: "Awooooo. Awooooo. Awooooo."

Chapter 7

Wolf-Bitten

Rangeen's farewell to her daughter was a hug and two kisses, each on one cheek, and a whisper in the ear: "Pspspspsps."

Jan had heard many of those whispers during the days he spent in the Old City with the Old Dame. One more whisper could not possibly hurt, he admitted. Maybe she had advised her daughter to behave herself; at least on the British land lest she would cause trouble for the good citizen Rangeen.

Yes, Jan thought the same. *Let it pass safely here and up there and then down there until we get back home. Then no matter if she would set fire to our house.*

But his hopes proved to be mere dreams. From the airport and until they got home, Vian doubled her abnormal conduct as if her mother's last instructions were orders to torture the already tortured husband.

They still hadn't reached the checkpoint when they were about to be kicked out of the airport. A long distance separated them from the air-stair when the airport police wanted to arrest them. They had flown less than fifteen minutes when the crew held tight to the pilot who wanted to jump out of the plane into the Mediterranean. And all the passengers were scolding Jan for not controlling his wife instead of scolding her for embarrassing her husband.

This proves my theory about feminism to be a system of superstitions, he thought. *The man is responsible for everything… everything. To my bad luck.*

"Did your mom whisper a magic spell in your ear?" Jan asked her, testing the practice that was globally accepted as superstition.

"Why? Did I do anything wrong?" she asked in turn.

It became useless. It was always useless.

Finally, came the last weird, inexplicable, unexpected, but the less harmful thing. Vian messaged Dana to bring the car to the airport, leave the keys on the engine, and leave the airport without looking over his shoulder to ask 'why'.

Vian sent the message and rested her back on the seat, smiled, and shut her eyes.

She wants to drive home, Jan thought. *Why? I may ask, of course without looking over my shoulder like Dana. Perhaps even she, herself, doesn't know. But driving the car and making it run under a heavy truck is better than the pilot blowing up the plane.*

He looked at her, unbelieving his awful wish. But her face wasn't the kind of how people expressed themselves when they thought of little things to do. Something awful was on its way.

Then it turned out to be a wrong estimation. After creating a few little troubles, starting from the plane door to the airport parking lot, Vian told him she wanted to drive just because she wanted to drive. She was missing driving, and that was all.

His unpredictable wife ran with light steps to the SUV, opened the driver's door, and jumped on the seat, joyfully bouncing on it.

Jan looked at the two bags he pulled and the two bags Vian left. He thought it to be unfair even for a porter, but immediately withdrew it.

You got over it unharmed, idiot, he said to himself. *Do you think that loading four bags into the car is a great loss?*

Then he remembered his dream.

The airport felt cold those thirty minutes after sunset. The general atmosphere reminded him of ghosts and vampires. But Vian was calm. And smiling. And then singing.

The car left the last checkpoint at the airport. Vian drove down the highway that ran along the chain-link fence of the airport.

To push the bad expectation away from his head, Jan counted the metal posts: One. Two. Three. Four. Four or five. Say five. Whether four or forty, am I going to pay anything? We've left many behind, but say six. Who cares?

Then it began to bother him. Then his eyes rolled. And nausea. Vomiting would follow.

Stop looking at the fence! Pray Vian would bump into the heaviest truck on the highway! Just stop it!

He forced himself to look ahead. A merciless tinnitus beat his ears.

"Are you okay, my dear?" Vian asked, smiling and not turning eyes from the road.

"Oh, yes, fine, oh, yes, yes, fine, oh," he reiterated like a bewildered man who thought that repeating the words would drive back the marching vomit.

Now she turned to him. She saw the fence running backward.

"Too little facilities in the airport compared to its huge area of land," she said.

"Oh, yes, right, oh, yes, yes," Jan said.

"Jan!" she yelled.

"What?"

"The dark plain is inspiring."

Jan swallowed to pull the sour stomach soup inside.

"The dark what is doing what?" he asked, his eyes still rolling. "Oh, yes, yes. Inspiring. Inspiring of what? Sickness?"

She didn't answer and made a sharp angle to the unpaved shoulder of the road on the right and drove on it. The headlights lit the corner of the fence that they needed less than a minute to reach. A sudden slowing down and then a tighter ninety-degree turn to the right. The car moved on a dirt road along the other side of the fence.

Jan's eyes stopped rolling and they stood out. In a moment, he forgot the sickness he tried to dispel. It was another craziness, but he sensed the wisdom of treating it with some indifference.

"I… I think this's the wrong way home, Lulu," he told Vian, who grabbed the driving wheel firmly and pressed her lips together.

"I know," she answered, opening a little slit of her mouth to say it. "Home is ninety degrees to our left."

Jan thought of what to say. He found something trivial. He was about to say it when Vian made a sudden break and turned off the engine and the headlights. She opened the glove box.

"I'm sure Dana keeps the cigarettes he secretly smokes here," she said.

"Oh, you came here to smoke," Jan said. "But you could've smoked while driving. It's not forbidden. I can swear on it on behalf of the traffic police."

"You know I hate smoking," she said while leaning over Jan's knees and disturbing the glove box to find the object she needed. Jan looked at her hand.

"Besides, the watching towers will see the burning cigarette," he said as if he hadn't heard her explaining she didn't want to smoke.

Vian found the object and held it before his face. It was a lighter. She ignited it. The low sound of the click made Jan jerk.

"I should change my name to Jan Jerkinson," he said.

"I wanted this," she said while opening the door and getting out.

She walked along the fence until her silhouette almost vanished in the darkness. Jan got out and followed her. He saw her gathering sticks and hay in a little pile.

"Don't, please," Jan implored. "It's dangerous. The airport is on the other side of this revealing fence."

"What if the airport is there?" she asked, simply.

"Surveillance cameras are watching," he answered, one step away from weeping. "Tough security men will rush here. Merciless dogs will join them. You know I'm not a fan of dogs, even harmless Milo."

"Let them all rush here," she said, igniting the lighter under the sticks. "We're outside their area."

"We're close to their area," he kept imploring. "They may think we're terrorists giving signals to fellow terrorists."

Jan looked over his shoulder as if a security force was just behind them. Vian sat on the ground, pulled up her knees, and stretched her arms to the fire. The white smoke went up. A mild gush of air blew and pushed it to Jan's face. He coughed.

"Surrounded By Misery." He remembered the title of his life story he wanted to write but he never started it. He only picked the title and it meant everything. He remembered he wanted to print it with all blank pages and one sentence: "Write down your misery in the blank pages and I bet it won't be worse than mine."

He moved back to the car. This time he would let her down.

If the security men came, let them arrest her. Let them shoot her to death. No. Let them shoot her in the leg. Not useful. The problem is with her hands. And her brain. And her tongue. Yes, shoot her in the tongue. And in the hand.

Shoot two places and get another free: in the leg. One leg, please. She needs the other for her house duties.

Jan was managing to continue his inner dialogue when he suddenly shouted:

"Oh, here it came!"

"Who came, my dear?" Vian asked, calmly and hugged her knees. "The security men?"

"No. The wolves," Jan answered, unable to shout louder because he swallowed hard.

He ran back to the spot.

"Hurry up!" he yelled. "Get into the car! The wolves. The wolves!"

Vian stretched her arms to the fire. She slowly turned to him.

"Calm down," she said. "They're dogs, not wolves."

"No. No. Wolves," he yelled. "Don't you hear? Awooo. Dogs don't howl awooo."

She looked at the fire and said nothing. Jan grabbed her armpits by his hands from behind and tried to make her stand to her feet.

"Even if they're dogs. They seem savage," he said, nearly crying. "There are no security men with them to leash them."

The howling got closer. It was like a storm rushing toward them. Vian looked in that direction.

"Wolves in this area?" she asked, almost whispering. "And in such time of the year when it's cold but no snow had fallen to block the country?"

Still leaning forward and his hand under her armpits, Jan looked up at the attacking pack.

"Oh, yes. They're wolves," he said, slowly.

He remembered a movie he watched. The protagonist drove the wolves away with a burning branch of a tree.

If my bad luck is a reality, he thought, *then the movie was a lie.*

Bad luck came from another corner. The fire was only half-burning little sticks. He pulled Vian by the armpits. Now scared, she crawled back on her butt and pushed the ground with her feet.

"Help me up to my feet," she screamed.

"I'm trying," he screamed back. "Get your butt from the ground."

The pack was a few hundred meters away. She suddenly jumped to her feet and ran to the car. Jan lost balance and fell on his back. Feeling his legs unable to help him stand up, he lay on his face and crawled toward the fire.

Vian had got into the car. She pressed the honk repeatedly to frighten the wolves. Jan thought she was encouraging him. He pushed away the burning sticks in the direction of the wolves. The sticks moved less than one meter away. The instinct of survival gave him the strength to grab one stick and throw it at the pack. Then the second and the third. The rest were but faintly burning cinders.

Vian kept honking. Then she remembered she could run over the animals. She drove the car toward them. Jan jumped to his feet when the car was about to hit him. Vian drove in spirals. The wolves avoided the car and howled at it. Jan followed the car until it braked. He couldn't open the door. Vian pushed the automatic lock button although the door wasn't locked. One of the wolves got closer. Jan kicked back.

Vian threw a bottle at him. He picked it up.

"I'm not thirsty!" he shouted.

"It's pepper spray!" Vian shouted back.

Jan stretched his arm with the spray.

"I won't let you rape me, bastard," he said from between his teeth.

But the spray couldn't drive the wolf away.

"It's expired!" he shouted.

"Sorry, darling," Vian shouted back. "It's paprika."

Jan sprayed some of it on his left palm and tasted it.

"Yes, it is. Awooo!"

He threw the bottle at the wolf that had bitten him and shouted again in pain.

The wolf didn't let loose his leg. Jan's pain turned into rage. He turned around and pushed two fingers into the wolf's eyes. The animal wailed and let go of the man's leg. And before another wolf got close to the fight, Jan pulled the door open, got in, and shut the door with a bang. He stayed a while groaning and twisting in his seat. The wolves were circling the car and jumping on and down the front hood. Vian looked at them, now with a blank face. She turned to her husband.

"Does it hurt, my dear?" Vian asked, calmly as she was used to doing.

Jan gaped. Then he shut his mouth.

"No, it doesn't," he answered. "I'm singing myself a song and dancing on the spot. Drive home."

"I can't," she said. "I'm freezing."

"Then let me drive."

"No. Not when you're like this."

"Then I'll sleep for a while."

And he fell asleep before she could object.

Vian remained freezing in horror. Jan woke up. He thought he had slept for a long time for he felt relieved. But the wolves were still howling and trying to break in.

"I feel I can drive," he said. "No. I feel I'm dying to drive. Have you ever felt you were dying to drive?"

"Then let's exchange seats," Vian said, ignoring his question.

She moved to the passenger's seat and he to the driver's. She got ready to jump onto the passenger's seat. He rolled his hands around her waist.

"Well?" Vian asked.

"Well," Jan answered.

"It isn't the right place for romantic feelings," she said. "The wolf on the front hood is watching us. Besides, you never know what romantic feelings are."

"That was before the wolf's bite," he said, his eyes blazing with what Vian felt as a savage look.

"Jan!" she said.

He snarled.

Vian shut her eyes. "You're scaring me," she said.

"Did you say I never knew what romantic feelings are?" he asked.

"Yes," she answered. "You used to say it shyly."

"And when you hadn't any reaction, I used to whimper like a wounded dog," he said.

She nodded.

"That was before," he said, lifting her to the passenger's seat. "And the word 'before' has died tonight."

"Will you explain it to me?" she asked, as guileless as a child.

"I'll explain it practically when I show you how I'd deal with those bastards outside," he said, scrawling on his butt to the driver's seat.

He turned to the back seat, pulled it downward, and took the jack handle.

"Don't be silly," Vian told him.

He turned to her, frowning, waved the rod, and opened the door. Vian tried to grab him by the jacket but he twitched and got out. He kicked the door back shut. With all his might, he beat the wolf standing on the hood with the rod. The wolf wailed and fell.

Jan pointed to his bandaged forehead with the other hand.

"Don't you see this?" he shouted at the wolf. "I'm the man who used to hurt every wall and door that refused to obey my wishes."

The closest wolf jumped to him. He struck it with a circular swing of the rod.

"And the wardrobe," he shouted.

The wolf wailed.

The third received a blow on the head.

"And the floor," he shouted again.

Then the fourth, on the side of the neck. Vian was gaping and covering her mouth with both hands. She didn't hear him snarling, but she saw what looked like a fire in his eyes.

When Jan beat the fifth until the seventh wolves, the pack, all hurt, began to move back facing the man. Then all withdrew and ran away. Jan pierced the rod into the dry mud. He looked up at the dark sky and let out a loud laugh.

"Hahahaha!"

He moved to the car, popped open the driver's door and grinned at Vian.

"Dude, I never thought this crazy dream would come true so darn fast," he told her. "Nor imagined it would turn out like this."

Headlights of approaching, rushing cars shone from the airport side. Jan got into the car at ease and rolled the window down. He turned on the engine and drove away from the spot. He stuck his head out the window and let out a hearty howl:

"Awooooo!"

"Jan! You didn't explain what's happening to you," Vian said.

He brought his head back inside, pressed his chin against his throat, and pouted.

"From now and on, you call me 'Jan After the Bite'," he declared.

Then burst into a guffaw, "Haha. Hahaha. Hahahahaha."

PART TWO

JAN AFTER THE BITE

Chapter **8**

A Wolf in the House

Jan refused to go to the hospital. Nothing was wrong with him, he told Vian. He feared that something indeed was wrong with him and that the doctor would prescribe a medication that could undo the effect of the wolf's "medicine."

The wolf had healed him, he judged, but the doctors would take him back to his normal position which was only a U-turn back to the way of destruction. Doctors would then be happy they did all they could do while Jan would curse them with all his heart.

He drove home. Vian called Dana and Tara to be ready to receive them. At the gate, Jan got out of the car and walked, limping, into the yard toward the entrance. On looking at his injured leg, he noticed that his jacket wasn't zipped. He zipped it and straightened. The jacket held his trunk tight.

Wow! he thought. *Iron chest, iron back, iron arms and shoulders. And I never felt my body so erected. It's like a reinforced 350 psi concrete column. Wow! Wow!*

Someone pulled the door open. The nanny appeared in the doorway, then Tara who pumped into her from behind and ran to the garden. She whooped, opening her arms to them for a hug. Jan received her with wide-opened arms and a firm smile. She skipped him and collided with her mother. Vian lifted her and kissed her on the cheeks. Jan's arm stayed splayed out. His smile turned into a mocking one.

When it's a fun time, she wants me to play with her, he thought to himself. *When it's serious, she runs to her mother. Wait for me! I'll make all your days serious. She wants me to play with her! Bah!*

He continued his way to the entrance with his hug ready for his son. Dana stayed unmoving in the doorway.

"Hi, Dad. Hi, Mom. Welcome back," Dana said with a failed attempt to show interest.

Jan lowered his arms.

No, he thought, *I'm no more going to beat objects with my head. That time's over, folks. And as to you, bastard, I'll beat your empty head with mine.*

He moved through the doorway. Dana stepped aside to let him in. Although there was room for both, Jan beat Dana's right shoulder with his left.

"Awoo," Dana cried and put his hand on his shoulder.

He stared at his father who kept limping inside without apologizing or seeming to be hurt. Dana noticed his father's leg, but since it was none of his business, he didn't want to bother him asking about it. Tara, too, noticed it when she came inside. Her mother was throwing an arm around her shoulder.

"What's wrong with your leg, Dad?" she asked. "Did a wolf bite it?"

Jan stopped, stayed unmoved for a while, and then turned around to face her.

"How fast you told her about it," he told Vian.

Vian opened her eyes wide and lifted her shoulders. Then she lowered them and pouted and shook her head.

Tara released her mother's hand from her shoulder, darted toward her father, pulled his jacket, and looked up at him.

"I saw it in a dream last night, Dad," she said.

"Hmm, Mmm, Emm," Jan mumbled with surprise.

"Yes, Dad, I saw it," she said.

"Dream, eh?" he asked her, then he showed her his teeth. "Then you all will be dreaming of things that have passed forever and you'll wish if they come back."

"Milo!" Tara called for the dog.

The dog came out of Tara's room and ran to the girl. It stopped halfway.

"Here's the dog with the standard, non-unique name; Milo," Jan said. "Howdy, Googy? I've come across a cousin of you. But he was a haughty noble, not a dirty Googy."

Milo barked twice at Jan who looked at it with contempt. The dog wanted to bark the third when it saw Jan's eye now blazing. Jan then snarled at it. The dog retreated two steps and sat on its hind legs. It shrank and shivered, looked up at Jan, and whimpered.

"Go back inside, Milo," Tara ordered the dog.

Milo turned around, bowed its head, and trudged back to the room. Jan smiled from the corner of his mouth.

"Why did you call it Milo?" he asked Tara.

"You've asked me this a hundred times," Tara replied.

"Hundred and one," Jan said. "Wasn't there a name for such dirty creatures in our language?"

"A name like what?" Tara asked.

"Like, let's say; Dana," Jan answered.

"We already have one," Tara said.

"Then Dana Two," Jan said.

Dana looked sideways at his father.

"Something feels off on this weird night," he said.

"Night, weird or normal, is the right time for only one thing," Jan said.

"Oh, Jan, stop it!" Vian said.

Jan turned to her. "I didn't mean the thing you imagined," he said. "I'll say that one later."

He turned back to Dana whose eyes were rolling.

"Didn't you know the fact that night is the work time for vampires?" he asked him.

Vian sighed with relief. Then she took Jan's arm by the hand and smiled.

"Wolves never can bite vampires," she said. "It's vampires who bite everybody. Let's go to our bedroom and take a rest."

They went in. It was Dana's turn to sigh.

"What a long night it was," he said to Tara who understood nothing.

Once in their bedroom, they sat on the edge of the bed.

Vian pressed her right side to Jan's left and rolled her hand around him. She leaned her head and rested her cheek on his arm, then shut her eyes and smiled.

"Oh, how wonderful!" she said.

"Yes, it's wonderful to be back to one's din… I mean, home," he said, not sure she meant it.

"Oh, no," she said. "How wonderful to have such a hard-featured husband."

Still smiling, she raised her head to him.

"Did you know that you are taller than me?" she asked.

"No, I didn't," he answered. "I mean not until now."

"Does wolves' saliva contain growth hormones?"

"Maybe growth. Certainly madness, I guess," he replied. "I never came across short, mad people. They're wiser than tall people."

"You're taller now," she said.

"Maybe I was before," he said. "But I used to bow and stoop and follow you like a slave that no man could free, Delilah."

"Right, Tom," she said. "And that was why you always looked shorter than me."

"It became history," he said, freeing his chest and standing up.

He moved to the middle of the room, stopped and puffed out his chest wide, and grinned.

"History always has turns and twists, ups and downs," he declared in an authoritative voice. "And this is my up time."

He grinned broader and his eye shone.

"I'm up, up, up," he yelled. "Hahaha. Hahaha. Bahahahaha."

He ended the guffaw, looked up at the ceiling, and howled in a low voice, "Awoooo!"

Chapter 9

Revenge

The next morning at the breakfast table, Jan and Vian waited for Dana and Tara to join in. Jan wore trousers and a shirt. Vian ran her hand over Jan's sleeve.

"You're handsome in these," she said. "But isn't it more comfortable to wear pajamas?"

Jan straightened his bent elbow to let Vian run her hand up and down his arm.

"I won't bring shame to my race by wearing pajamas on my first wolfish day," he replied. "A wolf in pajamas! Huh! And stripped pajamas like those of the retired Director General!"

Tara came first and sat at the table. She rubbed her haunches at the chair to get balanced on it. Dana came after a while.

The few first minutes passed without the family engaging in a conversation.

Tara was turning her eyes between her parents. Jan noticed her glances.

"Want to say something, kid?" Jan asked her in a voice that made him feel like a cowboy in a western movie.

"Yes," Tara replied. "Why were you beating Mom the last night?"

"I wasn't beating anybody," he answered. "I still didn't take office as Beater-in-Chief. But don't worry. I'll do it soon. I'll do very soon."

He balled his right fist and opened it.

Tara insisted, "But mom was screaming."

Dana's head sank into his shoulders. Vian half shut her eyes and pressed her lips.

"I told you, Jan," she scolded him as softly as she could.

"See, Dad? Mom told you not to beat her," Tara said.

Dana sank in his seat and looked down at the table.

"Stop it, idiot," he whispered to Tara. "It's an eighteen-plus-plus planned affair."

Jan turned to him.

"And you're an eighteen-minus-minus random affair," he told him. "How old are you, boy?"

"Physically, fifteen," Dana answered, fiddling with his spoon.

"I told you, Jan," Vian repeated.

"Mom told you, Dad," Tara said.

Jan thudded his knife at the dish.

"And why didn't you come to rescue your mom when you heard her screaming?" he asked Tara.

Tara straightened in her chair. "I did," she said in a sharp voice. "I beat your room door and shouted to you to open up."

"I was so busy licking my injury that I heard nothing," her father said. "And what did your brother do?"

"He pulled me by the arm back to my room," Tara replied.

"Good boy," Jan said. "You know your job well. Do it again when you hear your mother screaming."

"I told you, Jan," Vian said again.

"Mom told you, Dad," Tara said.

"Okay," Jan said. "You don't even know what your mom told me."

He turned to Dana, whose eyes were rolling.

"Why don't you tell your sister about it?" Jan asked him, smiling from the corner of his mouth.

"Oh, no… well… well…," Dana mumbled.

Jan turned to his daughter.

"Okay for the second time," he told her. "I won't beat her. At least when you are both at home. Did you hear, Dana?"

"Oh, yea... yeah," Dana mumbled again, now lightly beating the omelet with the spoon.

"When you get married," Jan told him, "you must do like I did. No begging. No whimpering. And you stop humiliating yourself or you'll end up gaining nothing and then you'd curse your bad luck whereas you should curse your bad butt."

Dana swallowed. He looked at Tara to see if she understood anything. The smile on Tara's face while chewing on her food told him she still waited for her father to explain his beating her mother.

Thank God, Dana thought. *Her usual foolish features.*

Jan took the napkin that he didn't use, wiped his hands with it, and beat the table with it.

"That's enough for this morning," he said in an authoritative voice. "Everybody goes about his and her work. This includes dirty Milo."

Tara pressed her lips with discontent, stood up, and went to her room. Dana followed to his. Vian leaned her head on Jan's shoulder and smiled.

"I told you, Jan," she said.

"Whether you tell me or tell them, they have to get used to it," Jan said.

He ran his hand in her hair.

"Well, Vivi, won't you go about your work?" he asked.

"You're my work," she answered.

He scratched her head with his fingertips.

"Want to go shopping this morning?" he asked. "I'd like to go out. Not for shopping as I hate it, you know."

"Anything you like," she said. "But why not shopping?"

"You know what shopping for me means; oh, it should now be 'meant,'" he said. "I should revise my verb tenses. So, it meant torture. That was in the past, to explain the linguistic information more. I still hate shopping, to add more information. Moreover, I feel that going to markets is a shameful job for a wolf. I just want to go to beat some people there."

"Alright," Vian said. "I mean no, don't beat anybody."

"Only those whom I hated or those who didn't respect me."

"Okay, just snarl at them. But before shopping, let's visit the doctor."

"Wow! Wolf's blood is so strong you became pregnant after only a few hours," he said. "I want twin wolves if you don't mind. A boy and a girl."

She lightly slapped him on the shoulder.

"Jan! The doctor's for you," she said.

"Why should I need a doctor?" he asked. "Men don't bear babies. Let alone male wolves. Or you began to abandon conservative beliefs?"

"Not for this," Vian said. "The people whom I know say that if a dog bites a man he'll live only a few days."

"Ah, I see," he said. "But it wasn't a dog. Besides, the other people whom you don't know say that if a wolf bites a man, he'll be promoted to the rank of nobles and woodslords."

He lifted his hands and head.

"Waooo. We have the noblest blood on Earth," he said.

"What if it was a hybrid wolf?" she asked.

Jan scratched his chin. "You mean a cocktail of a noble wolf and a dirty dog?" he asked.

"Or a wolf and a dirtier hyena," she said.

"Hyena? Ugh! Give me that dish over there to vomit in it."

"The doctor can find out if it was this or that," she said.

"Well, can the doctor also extract the blood of this or that inferior, meritless animal?"

"She can."

"She?!" Jan exclaimed. "Sorry, madam. I don't trust female doctors. At least, since yesterday night."

"Naza is a competent doctor. Believe me."

Jan leaned his neck to the left and scratched the right side with his forefinger.

"Let me decide after doing your shopping," he said. "Go get dressed. Hurry up!"

Vian smiled and jumped to her feet. Jan stayed alone. He was so pleased with his new status that he circled his mouth and howled mutely. Then he balled his right fist tight and beat the table.

"I'll go to the outside world and teach them lessons in respecting our genus," he said. "I'll begin with Vian's favorite shopkeeper. That worthless bootlicker who always ignored me because he knew that Vian, not I, is who decides on what to buy and also because he could cheat her."

Vian didn't delay. She hurried to the door. Jan stayed sitting in his place. Vian opened the door. Half of her body was in the doorway when she suddenly halted and then slowly turned around to Jan who seemed not to be pleased with the situation. She nodded as to say she understood. Bending and stretching her hand to one side in invitation, she stepped aside to let him go first.

Jan walked toward the door with both hands in his jacket pockets. He stepped into the doorway. Vian placed her hands on his shoulders from behind, smiled with all her face, and bounced in her place with joy like a child.

When getting into the car, Vian wanted to get into the driver's seat as usual but she retreated at once. She cocked her head to one side, stretched her hand with the keys to Jan, and bent her knees down.

Jan inserted his little finger into the ring of the keys, took the keys from her, and revolved them with his finger. Smiling and slightly limping, he took Vian's arm by the hand, circled the car to the passenger seat, and opened the door for her. Vian got in, smiling. Jan banged the door. Vian jerked. Jan went back to the other side of the car and got in.

"Sorry, Vivi," he said.

"It's okay, strong man," Vian said, still smiling.

Jan drove. He skipped three clothes shops Vian asked him to stop by. It amazed him that Vian wasn't bothered with his repeated refusals. He thought he owed her an explanation.

"I want our first destination to be the market that I hate its owner more than I hate jeans torn at the knees," he said.

"Every word you say is an order to be obeyed, darling," she said. "But please don't harm him. We don't want to spoil your first wolfy day."

"It's the guy's day that will be spoiled," Jan said.

He pulled up the car before the market and got out. Vian delayed to walk behind him. He grabbed her arm and pulled her to make both walk side by side. She pressed her upper arm with his, looked at him, and smiled.

At the door, Vian stopped to let Jan enter first. He held out his arm toward the door.

"Wolves' wives first," he said.

She entered with a broad smile on her face to show she was proud of her husband. The shopkeeper hurried to receive her.

"How lovely to see you again," he said, using the singular form of 'you' in their language. "I guess you were abroad." He used the singular form again.

Vian nodded.

Although the man saw Jan coming behind her, he chattered with Vian for a while. Jan watched him with his fists clenched in his pockets. Finally, he coughed.

The shopkeeper moved his head away from Vian's body to see who it was.

"Oh, Jan. Nice to see you," he said and went on his conversation with Vian.

"I'm called Mister Jan, dummy fish," Jan said.

Jan's words surprised the man. He stopped talking and stayed silent for a while.

Jan addressed Vian, "Make your shopping quickly and let's get out of this stinky place."

The shopkeeper didn't miss Jan's dry voice. He looked at Vian with a question in his eyes. Vian was smiling and her eyes didn't show any surprise.

"No, Mister Jan," the man said. "My place isn't stinky."

"Yes, it is," Jan said. "I think you're letting loose tons of hydrogen sulfide gas at the morning shift and other tons in the evening. What do you eat? Trucks of onions?"

Vian smiled.

"Jan!" she said with a mild protest.

"I'm serious," Jan said. "I forgot to bring a mask. Do you have masks, Mister H2S?"

"Oh, Jan!" Vian said again.

"It's okay, madam," the man said, "Mister Jan seems to be upset because of something."

"Never," Jan said. "It's only the mass production of hydrogen sulfide from your deep tunnel that ends with a lidless hole."

Vian moved to do her shopping while the man was drying the sweat off his face amid Jan's comments.

The spouse left the place with the shopkeeper not following them outside as he used to do. Both noticed it.

"You made the man stay inside for his safety," Vian said.

"Yes, and he's now licking the glass door instead of our asses."

Two young workers followed them with the stuff they had bought. Jan opened the trunk for them. They placed them in it and stayed unmoving. Vian understood.

"Give them something, Jan," she said.

"Why should I?" Jan asked. "It's their duty. It's not a custom in our city."

Then he snarled. The two young men shared a glance. Jan regretted it.

"Or, I tell you both something?" he said, smiling. "Take this."

He handed them a big money bill.

"Wolves are generous creatures," he told them. "And tell your boss to be less generous with his abdominal emissions."

While driving, Jan turned to his wife with a smile from the corner of his mouth.

"How was that?" he asked.

"You've surprised all three of them," she replied.

Jan nodded. "And also frightened the first of them," he said. "And this was the important part of it."

"Oh, I should go the next time alone," she said.

"The next time when you go alone, he'll offer you sincere respects and will lick your shoes when you leave. Tell him that I'll check your shoes to make sure he shined them well. Otherwise, I'll go and beat him."

They entered a crowded street.

"How about this?" Jan asked.

"Lots of people," Vian answered.

"No, I mean how about parking the car and then dragging you by the hair like the caveman and his wife while the dinosaurs watch and nod their approval?"

"Wow! I'd love to," Vian replied. "But unlike the dinosaurs, those people who lack imagination and romance will misinterpret the situation."

Jan lifted his right hand from the wheel and scratched his chin, showing the right corner of his jaws.

"I need a time machine to go back to old, lovely eras," he said, whistling then a medley of quick music of howls.

C h a p t e r 10

Marketing the Wolf

Vian repeated her suggestion that she and Jan go to the doctor, this time to find out if there was something in his genetic makeup that might have caused the recent transformation. Jan shook his head.

"I'm content this way," he said. "Aren't you content this way too?"

"Yes, but I want to make sure if lycanthropy is in your blood," she replied.

"I don't think so," he said. "There are no men in my family tree with long fangs. You know I joined the wolf club by acquisition, not by birth. That is, I'm a self-made wolf."

"We have nothing to lose if we go," she said.

"Yes, we will lose the doctor's fee," he said. "And perhaps your friend, the doctor, will provoke me with her questions about my unsavory past and force me to bite her."

"Don't worry," she said. "I told you she's skilled. Naza is my friend and she won't get angry if you nibble her."

"I like that you're loyal to your underachieving friends and want to find work for them," he said. "But, I won't go. I'll send her the visit fee with a lock to shut her clinic, and I'll give the key to a cow to swallow it."

"Alright, forget about Naza," she said. "Let's go to my other friend. She'll inform Naza about our visit details."

"And who is she?" he asked. "Another loser looking for clients?"

"She's Nasreen, the social researcher," she answered.

"And the feminist activist," added Jan.

Vian closed her eyes and opened them. Jan raised his eyebrows in refusal.

"You know how much I hate man-hating feminists before and after my wolfish transformation?" he said. "I won't satisfy myself by only biting her; I'll tear her apart with my fangs and claws."

He bared his teeth and extended his fingers. His nails were freshly trimmed. He pulled his hands back and put them in his pockets.

"My fangs are enough," he said.

"I won't stop you," she said.

"Really?"

She shook her head downward with quick movements. Jan awkwardly mimicked her head motion in acceptance.

At the reception of the social researcher's clinic, Jan's mouth moved to one side in a mocking smile. He read the tablet aloud:

"Nasreen Sigmund Freud The Thirteenth, Psychiatrist specialist in stealing money from clients and then convincing them to commit suicide to cover up her robbery."

The reception was empty.

"Didn't I tell you?" Jan said to Vian. "All the clients killed themselves, including Nasreen's receptionist."

Vian knocked on the door and entered without permission. Jan followed.

He whispered to her, "I knew she was ugly, but I didn't imagine she'd be this beyond standard. She's a typical feminist activist." Jan intentionally spoke the last sentence loud enough for the researcher to hear.

"Thank you," said Nasreen, smiling as if she was frowning.

After exchanging perfunctory greetings; unsuccessfully intended to be warm and sincere, Vian explained her husband's condition to Nasreen. Half the details were unreal. Jean pondered the reason for that. Vian's description of the wolfish state dominated over other topics. And as if Vian was pleased with this, she described the situation with a broad smile, looking more at her husband than at the researcher.

Nasreen caught Vian off guard with a direct question that interrupted her enthusiastic presentation.

"Was your husband ideal before that condition?"

Jan pressed his lips together. "Ah, here begins the unscientific journey of interventions," he said. "What's your definition of an ideal husband?"

"That's well-known," the researcher answered, dryly.

"No, it's not even half-known," Jan said. "The definition of an ideal man doesn't fall within the realm of science but ideology. For example, your ideal man is the submissive one who nods like a fool to all the delirium of feminist activists."

"The ideal man isn't someone dominating over women," the researcher sharply responded. "Besides, I am the researcher, and I determine definitions and standards."

"And we men aren't obliged to accept your definitions and ravings," he said.

The researcher turned to Vian with a frowning face.

"What do you think?" she asked.

"Oh, he's a strong man in every sense of the word," Vian said. "We can't impose our views on strong men."

"Well, take him and have your fill," Nasreen said.

"Calm down a bit," Vian said. "I want to know the reason for his condition and if it will last." She uttered the word "his condition" as if she were flirting with her husband.

"So, was your husband fierce before this condition?" the researcher inquired.

"Before and after," Vian replied.

And what about my head, full of bruises in that "before"? Jan said to himself. *This fakes my shameful history. But it's okay since the situation requires it. When I get home, I'll apologize to every wall and piece of furniture I've hit with my head.*

"But what I know is otherwise," Nasreen said to Vian, nervously tapping her notebook with a pen.

Jan furrowed his eyebrows. "Enough of that," he told her.

"I wasn't talking to you," Nasreen said.

"I mean, stop hitting the notebook with the tip of your pen," Jan said. "You're reminding me of something."

Nasreen turned to Vian. "Didn't I tell you I knew he wasn't fierce before now?" she said, returning to tapping her notebook, this time enjoying it.

"So why do you ask me?" Vian asked.

"Because you're part of the situation," Nasreen answered.

Vian's eyes narrowed, with displeasure appearing on her pursed lips despite her usual smile.

"Sorry?" she asked.

The researcher ignored the question and continued her inquiry about Jan and the spouses' family relationship. Jan noticed that his wife's last concern was to find a cure for him, and the researcher's first concern was to find what would convict him. He also noticed that her face constantly changed from one color to another like a rainbow.

When both women finished, Nasreen arched her eyebrows, preparing to confront Vian with her husband's transformation.

"It's just the shock he suffered from the wolf's bite," she told her. "The shock will go away after a while and he'll return to his normal state."

Jan didn't like the explanation.

"This theory was entirely rejected," he firmly said. "One hundred and ten percent of scientists discarded the fateful bite theory since the nineteenth century because it wasn't aristocratic enough. They were one hundred and twenty percent certain that it was suitable only for commoners. And suitable also for social researchers who, due to their idleness, sleep until noon and then work as feminist activists in the afternoon and then sleep in their office because there are no interested visitors."

"I don't care about your opinion or the opinions of other men, even if they are one hundred and thirty percent of the population," Nasreen said without looking at him. "My life follows the theories I believe in."

"And this's another proof of my theory about feminists," Jan said, this time in a voice that he wanted to be low, but it came out audible. "Most of them are failures in their social lives, and many of them are ugly. The beautiful ones among them will get married or become models and forget all their previous nonsense."

This was more than Nasreen could bear. She turned to him angrily, then to Vian.

"Your husband should hold his tongue," she said to Vian.

Vian leaned on Jan's shoulder, placed her hand on him, and smiled.

"Oh, he's handsome when he speaks like this," Vian said. "He looks like a lone wolf in a snow-covered forest."

Jan was puzzled. So, his wife didn't come here to find out the reason for his condition. He thought that the current situation deserved supporting his wife by adding something to her description of him.

"And howls on a snowy hill while the wolves respond without daring to approach him," he said, then howled in a low voice, "Awooo."

The session ended with what Jan considered proof of the researcher's complete failure. He still needed to make sure that Vian didn't intend to obtain information about his condition.

He inquired about it as they headed toward the parking lot.

"Of course, I didn't bring you for that reason," Vian said, tucking her arm into his and lowering her body slightly to make him appear taller than her.

"And you don't need treatment because you're not ill. You should remain like this."

Jan pressed his lips, opened his eyes, then his mouth.

"Huh?" he said, keeping his mouth agape.

"I brought you to my friend just for show," she said. "I wanted that loser to know who my husband is. Nasreen will mention our visit to Naza. Naza will tell Sozan. Sozan will tell Lana, and the whole gang of losers will know about it."

"Ah, now I understand. Like Milo, the dog that our daughter Tara takes to her friends to show off," he said. "Milo, the silly, dirty dog."

Vian placed her other hand on his shoulder and smiled, looking up at him.

"But you are the mighty wolf."

He smiled back with a stern face.

"I know," he said. "Do you want me to howl like the lone wolf on the snowy hill?"

She pressed her body to his shoulder as they continued walking toward the car.

"Yes, but when we get home," she said. "And strongly."

Jan smiled. "Yes," he said. "I love that 'strongly.'"

Then he lifted his head and moved it to the sides as if singing mutely.

Chapter I I

The Party

After presenting her husband in his new character to the social researcher and then indirectly to the group of specialists and her other friends, Vian became eager to introduce him to the rest of her acquaintances. She first proposed a party for thirty people in compensation for the canceled banquet before traveling with Jan to visit her mother. Jan told her that the feast was history and was over.

"Consider that all the documents of that party were burned in Persepolis by Alexander the Great along with the Zoroastrian religious books," he said.

Vian didn't insist.

"Well, let's set it aside," she said. "How about the New Year's party at the five-star hotel that the city sees from wherever it wants?"

"And you want me to climb on top of the tower and strip like Tarzan and scream like him?" Jan asked. "Oh, and on the occasion of the Western Pagan Year, did you know that Tarzan is the representative of Western civilization? Instead of teaching monkeys how to civilize and wear clothes, he got naked and made nudity a civilized value. You know I don't like the occasions belonging to the civilization of nudity. Also, as a patriotic wolf, I refuse to celebrate an occasion that is not ours."

"But a lot of patriotic people here celebrate it," she said.

"You mean fake patriots," he said. "They resemble the monkeys of Tarzan's forest who know nothing but imitating powerful Westerners. Tell you something? Postpone it to Nawroz."

"Oh, I can't wait until Nawroz," she said. "And there's no closer occasion."

"Yes, there is one in February," he said.

"Yes, right," she said. "It's Valentine's Day on the fourteenth of February."

"This too the monkeys imported from the forest of the strong people," he said. "I meant the demonstrations on the seventeenth of February against the corruption of the government, in which the corrupt killed a group of demonstrators."

"Are you serious? Who celebrates a day like this?"

"Well, there's an occasion closer. It's the tenth of December."

"What feast is that?"

"Feast of hypocrisy," he replied. "Every year they celebrate the Universal Declaration of Human Rights. We'll participate in a cultural forum and I'll tell the representatives of Western governments if they come to give us their false lectures, and most likely they won't come, that they use human rights against regimes that are not obedient enough. But when the regime is a good obedient, they reproach it just like they reproach their mistress when she doesn't groan as she should on the bed."

"Oh, Jan, what are these boring occasions?" Vian asked.

"Wolves only celebrate occasions like this," he said. "Can you imagine them celebrating an effeminate occasion like Valentine's Day?"

"And why not?"

"Do you want the wolf to carry a red rose and then when he wants to howl like a wolf herd leader he meows like a house cat? No. Our events must be violent."

"Which doesn't suit me," she said. "Find me a joyful occasion."

"How joyful?" he asked.

Vian snapped her thumb and middle finger and undulated, bending her knees.

"I want an event where there's dancing and singing," she answered, smiling.

"What's the use of that?" he asked. "You know I'm a hyper-conservative and I won't let you sing and dance."

"I'll dance with a group our national traditional dance, you national wolf."

"No way. Two men will hold your hands, each man from the side, and their body will rub against yours. I'll imagine testosterone flowing in their blood. No way for the second time. You women can't imagine how men feel. Masculine testosterone is ready for the slightest excitement as an attentive soldier and enthusiastic about his duty in an ambush. What did I tell you? I said no way. So it's no way for the third time."

"So I'll stand between two women."

Jan shook his head.

"Then a man comes with his belongings dangling between his thighs and gets stuck between you two and I'll have to beat him," he said. "Why do you insist on that occasion that coincides with the calendar of Christ's birthday but the Western Christians imitate the pagans with orgies and everything that Christ hated?"

"We also believe in Christ as a prophet," she said.

"We're more Christian than Westerners, my dear," he said. "They're secularists who apply only one verse from the words of Christ, which is, 'Render to God what is God's and to Caesar what is Caesar's,' and which I can swear he didn't mean in the sense they understand. They celebrate with Christ on the twenty-fifth of December and then one week later they forget Christ and celebrate with Satan."

"Well, I won't dance," she said. "I'll watch others dance."

Jan scratched his chin and pursed his lips.

"I agree if you promise to only watch," he said, then straightened his stance, and went on, firmly, "And for my part, I'll frown at those we know and who didn't respect me before. I'll also frown at those who don't know your husband to let them know him. Just as you're eager for an occasion to introduce *your me*, I'm also eager for an occasion to introduce *my me*."

Then he bared his fangs and turned his face to the sides. "Do I look like a real wolf?" he asked from between his teeth.

"Yes, yes, but don't bite anyone."

"Don't worry, I'm not stupid to bring another man to the Wolves Club," he said and then let a short laugh. "Ha! Imagine those worthless people turning into wolves. They deserve to be turned into dogs dirtier than Milo."

After they agreed to attend the party, Vian called her acquaintances and urged them to join them, even though it was early and no party had been announced at any hotel.

Then when the occasion was announced, Vian intensified her contacts to ensure the greatest number of attendees. Most of them were willing to come and see Jan in his transformation.

On the day of the event, the two were discussing what to wear. Jan insisted that Vian dress modestly while Vian insisted on him wearing a tie with the suit. Jan chuckled.

"Close your eyes and imagine a wolf sitting on his butt in front of a camera to take a photo to use for his passport. He wears a suit and a tie that hangs down to his stomach and tickles his navel. Ha-ha-ha. And transparent nearsighted glasses with a thick black frame. Ha-ha-ha."

"No, it's a bow tie," she said.

"Oh dear! A wolf with a bow tie! Ha-ha-ha! He'd look goofy wearing the glasses with thick, black frame."

"You're going to be handsome in it."

"I hate both thick and thin glasses. Ha! A wolf with glasses!"

"I mean, you're going to be handsome with a butterfly tie."

"Thanks for the clarification," he said. "I'll be a clown with it. Listen, this's my only offer: a suit of one color. Let's say black, and the jacket that's buttoned in the middle with just one button. I can negotiate the shirt, but a very light one, and without a tie. I'll then look like a man who came specifically to fight and then go home. And to prove it, I'll hold an unlit cigarette between my fingers. My hand holding the cigarette will be raised to my chest. No, between my chest and my stomach so that I point it down toward the personal belongings of everyone I hate. And all with a mocking smile at everyone around me. Of course, except for you, my dear Vivi."

Vian was finally convinced by her husband's offer, as what mattered to her was her husband's presence and their acquaintances seeing him. That night, she held his arm as they walked from the parking garage to the hotel entrance, then into the elevator, and finally into the ballroom.

On their way to their table, she smiled, bowed her knees slightly to look shorter than her husband, and turned her head left and right as if greeting the audience. When they arrived, their comments made her smile wider.

Before they sat at their table, they greeted those around them: Vian with artificial hugs and kisses, and Jan with a stern smile and a firm nod of the head from afar to the men as if he was butting them.

Less than a minute had passed after they sat down when Jan scratched the back of his right hand with his left.

"Did you drink something that made you allergic, my dear?" Vian asked, raising her voice with the words "my dear" to make others hear.

"Nothing," he replied. "We just came and haven't even breathed yet. My hand is itching to beat those around me because most of them didn't respect me."

"Forget them now," she said. "There'll come a better occasion when you can beat them all."

"Just as you didn't wait until Nawroz, I won't wait until the seventeenth of February," he said. "I'll start a fight as soon as possible tonight. How about that man who dyes his mustache and I think he's a senior official in the ruling party? Relatives of the victims of February seventeenth will rejoice to see him beaten and humiliated."

Vian poked her husband with her elbow and pointed her head toward the opposite end of the hall. The presenter had climbed the stage. He announced the beginning of the party with a local singer. The women screamed. Some men cheered. Jan looked at the singer mockingly. He was fat and had a large black mustache.

"Isn't that the one whose voice resembles a street vendor of uncooked sheep's head and trotters on a three-wheeled motorcycle?" Jan said, loudly enough for those next to them to hear.

Vian smiled. "He's a famous singer, honey," she said.

"Yes, but not as famous as cooked sheep's head and trotters," Jan said.

The first song was quiet. The singer then launched into a loud traditional song. The attendees, men and women, got up, held each other's hands in a row, and started the traditional collective dance. Jan gave a quick nod upward to the singer across from him.

"Look at how his veins rose like sewer pipes," he said. "He strains himself to sing with a pitch higher than his voice. He wouldn't have needed that if he shouted to sell raw head and trotters."

Then he blocked his ears with his index fingers.

"On top of that, it's an old worn-out song that no one left to sing," he added. "Even Milo sang it."

A man approached their table.

"Come on, Madam Vian, let's go to join the dance," he said.

Vian looked at her husband. Jan raised his head to the man with his fingers still in his ears. He shook his eyebrows up to the man to leave. The man frowned and left. Jan took his fingers out of his ears.

"A man who is not ashamed of his posterior," he said in a loud voice.

The man turned over his shoulder angrily. Jan shook his head up.

"Shoo, shoo," he said as if chasing away a chicken. "Your buttocks are so big you should've retreated, facing us instead of turning around to show it."

"Oh, don't be cruel, honey," Vian said, smiling.

Their neighbors exchanged glances. The singer had switched to a quieter song.

"Your husband doesn't seem to be getting along," a man said from afar. "I hope you can get along with him."

Jan looked at the man. He was the one Jan thought was a senior party official. Jan smiled mockingly from the corner of his mouth.

"Of course, you feel brave when you speak from behind two tables and five women," Jan told him. "Why don't you try to come closer and repeat your words here?"

Then he said to himself, "Yes, come here. The fight came faster than I imagined. Come over, you dyed mustache, to let me wipe its dye with my shoes."

The man frowned at Jan and seemed to be fidgeting in place. He turned back. His bodyguard was at the door, inattentive to him and watching the audience. The man decided to act on his own.

"Who do you think you are?" he shouted, hoping his guard would hear him.

"I'm your master and the son of the people," Jan replied calmly.

"No. You're my nut," the man said, angrily.

Jan turned to his wife.

"That's the one I told you I wanted to beat," he whispered to her. "I'll make it a double party."

"No, my dear. I told you we don't want a fight here," Vian said with half a smile, not caring about the upcoming fight.

"On the contrary, this's the best place," Jan told her. "A lot of people will see us and there'll probably be a camera. Or should I tell you? Take your phone and then post the next action movie. Hollywood will buy its rights from you for a million dollars."

Then he turned to the man.

"What did you say to me?" he asked him, his face exuding mockery. "I think you said I was your nut. It's a deal. It doesn't make a difference if it's the right or the left since this brings me closer to your wife when you're in bed together."

The man got up to his feet.

"You, dishonorable!" he shouted.

His wife grabbed his arm.

"Forget about him, Delovan," she said.

"Yes, forget about me, you the owner of a name teenagers have," Jan said. "Everyone named Delovan is too young to dye his mustache. Obviously, it's a pseudonym. Delovan! Hah! I think your real name is more like a salvo of farts."

The man tried to pull his hand out of the grip of his wife who remained holding it.

"Let go of my hand, I'll set him straight," he said to his wife.

"And why let go of your hand?" asked Jan. "She likes the idea of me being your nut close to her."

"He's dishonorable," the woman whispered.

"And since I'm your nut," Jan continued, "I'll be shaking every twelve o'clock at night with the chimes of the wall clock in the room next to your bedroom."

Instead of feeling jealous, Vian smiled with obvious joy.

"Enough of this, my dear, you've wiped the floor with him," she said, then looked with a smile left and right as if to say to those around her, "Look at my husband," and then took out her phone and started filming.

The man had got up and headed toward Jan's table. He stood near Jan, put his left hand on his waist, and shook his right hand and palm up so hard that his tie vibrated.

"Get up so I can teach you manhood," he said.

"And do you think manhood is having possessions that you don't use," Jan said and suddenly kicked the man on his testicles.

The man screamed, bent down, and grabbed his testicles. Jan put his elbow on the table.

"It won't make any difference with you," he told the man. "It wasn't worth anything anyway and no one would buy it from you if you thought of selling it."

The man turned around, hunching over and holding between his thighs.

"Turn toward me, that's to say toward your balls, you the guy with the dyed mustache," Jan said to him. "And since the occasion is the beginning of the Christian New Year, I should say: if they beat you on your right nut, turn your left one to them."

Delovan shook his head up toward the door.

The bodyguard had moved to the spot. Jan smiled mockingly, welcoming the next fight. The guard, who was wearing a black suit with a gun visible in the trouser belt under his jacket, pushed the stunned audience out of his way.

He reached the table and grabbed Jan's hair from behind. Jan poked the guard's stomach with his elbow. The man stifled a cry of pain and pulled Jan's hair tightly. Then he hit the table with Jan's head once and then again.

The man kept Jan's forehead and nose glued to the table. Jan stared at the table with bulging eyes and a convulsive face.

"No, not this one!" he shouted. "This crosses all red lines. It's a recall of the history of evil spirits before the airport fence era. No, no!"

He sprang to his feet and clenched his hands to the man's throat, shouting from between his teeth, "You have put your hand in the wolf's den, you trifle."

Before the man could reach for his gun, Jan grabbed his belt with the other hand and hoisted him overhead. He twirled twice, holding the man aloft above his head. Vian was smiling while filming with her camera.

"Get away from the table!" Jan shouted to her.

Vian got up and walked backward with light steps, still filming.

Jan threw the man on the table, which collapsed under his weight. Vian turned her phone to both sides to film the audience's reaction. The hall had fallen into chaos.

The hotel security rushed inside; then to stop before reaching the spot. Jan looked like a raging bull they should have avoided.

"Would you please, sir, come with us?" said one of them so politely that Jan felt it was coming straight from the heart.

Jan walked to Delovan, who stood stunned, grabbed the bottom of his jacket from behind, lifted it toward his neck, uncovering his shirt, and pushed him forward.

"This also comes with me," he said.

"Me too," Vian said.

"Stay here, ma'am," the security man said.

"No, he insulted my husband and called him his testicle," Vian said.

"Okay, but without filming," the security man said.

Vian raised her phone. "I've filmed the most important part here," she said. "If anything happens to my husband, I'll publish this to the world."

The security man pursed his lips.

"I bet she'll publish the footage immediately even if we give her husband a medal," he said in a low voice. Then he turned to the official.

"Did you hear, sir? I'd prefer you both work things out between yourselves."

"No way," the official said. "He hit me in the stomach."

"On his balls," Jan said. "They are who they are. Always lying."

The security man turned to Vian.

"Do you promise not to publish the video, ma'am?" he asked her.

"Mmmm," she said. "Okay. I'll cut off the part that belongs to the mister."

The security man turned to Delovan.

"What do you say, sir?" he asked him, his patience almost running out.

"Okay, let it all end," Delovan said. "But only for this moment and not forever."

"Better it ends forever," the security man said. "If anything happens to the mister in the future, people will repost the video and no one will ever forget it. Let me add, especially that they don't like officials. As you know, it's enough for someone to post something to make hundreds of them repost it."

Vian leaned on her husband's ear.

"This man is on our side," she whispered to him.

"When we're fighting with palace dogs, all are on our side, even the street dogs," Jan said.

"I'm so proud of you, Wolf," Vian whispered.

"You're so proud of me that you won't keep your promise and you'll publish the footage with a shoe logo and two crossballs," Jan said, feeling his forehead, now throbbing with pain from the blow

Chapter 12

The Wolf at the Peak of his Splendor

Vian set out to prepare a video of the party brawl to send to friends and relatives through private messages and to share it publicly with others. She made sure to remove the part in which Delovan's bodyguard hit Jan's head against the table. She asked Dana to do the deletion on his computer in an unnoticeable way.

Jan could hear them from the living room through the open door. He was looking at his forehead in a mirror on a table he had brought from the kitchen.

Dana shook his head.

"Impossible," he said. "The video was filmed with one camera, so cuts and fills will be noticeable. Unless I insert a clip in the place of the deletion."

Jan's mouth twisted into a mocking smile, tilting to one side.

"Cuts and fills! Huh!" he said. "This loser high schooler uses civil engineering terms."

"Like what?" Vian asked Dana.

"Like a commercial for an insecticide used for fights in five-star hotels and the protagonist himself tried it," he replied.

Jan felt the place of the blow on his forehead with the tip of his index finger as he looked in the mirror.

"That's one option," he shouted to his son. Then he said to himself, "Insecticide used for fights in five-star hotels, ..etc., etc. Now this boy is stealing my literary expressions. I must protect my intellectual property rights."

"Ask dad what else he wants," Dana said to his mother.

Jan heard him.

"Take this one," he shouted. "Put a picture of a rose in the place of the deleted part and type: 'A gift from heart to heart, and if you don't like our rose knock it off and return us the price' or type late congratulations on the new year that has passed: 'We forgot to congratulate you on it, but it's okay, you weren't interested anyway. Neither were we.' Or put a sign that says: 'It has been deleted in kindness to the faint-hearted who will die with or without this clip.'"

"All this doesn't work, dear," Vian shouted, then turned to Dana. "Insert a video clip from a footage one of the attendees has posted," she told him.

"People will know the clip isn't yours," Dana said, "and will ask why you used it."

"Well," Vian said. "In one shot, I turned the camera around the hall to record the audience."

"Yes, this works," Dana said. Then he whispered. "Although I prefer to leave the scene of beating my dad to keep him from becoming full of himself."

Jan felt that his son had said something bad about him.

"What did you say to your mom, boy?" he shouted at him.

"Nothing," Dana shouted back. "I just asked her if the location of the blow the official received could be shaded to avoid the social media marking it as pornographic."

"Oh, well," Jan said, then muttered to himself, complaining. "That's on the one hand. And on the other hand, there's this damn itch that insists on pinching me."

"Put a black banner over the scene where your dad beat the official," Vian told Dana, "and include the text: The fight against the official has been removed as per our agreement with him. Then make me another copy with the scene of the beating and write a sign at the beginning of the film saying that the version is for my dear friends and not for publishing."

"And then your dear friends will publish it," Dana commented.

"Sure," she said. "But not all of them. The envious women won't."

"It's okay, although this's a breach of your agreement with the official. I'm not the one who will pay the price. I promise to visit you in prison regularly and bring you the moldy mushroom soup you love."

Dana completed both copies of the film and sent them to his mother to post them. Vian went to her bedroom, lay on her stomach, and busied herself for an hour sending the full film to her private groups through private messages and then the curtailed film as a public post. Then she spent the rest of the day with housework and reading the reactions.

Jan watched the public film Vian sent him while still feeling in front of the mirror his forehead, which was getting worse. To his surprise, the place of the strike didn't turn blue. An old college lesson he remembered made him guess that the pressure from the blow was distributed over a wide area of his forehead. His attempt to convert the pressure to newtons per square failed, and then the same with pounds per square foot.

He shouted to Vian, "This damn itch is keeping me from enjoying my victory." Then he said to himself, "I may get the pressure value if I use grocery units like red watermelons or yellow pumpkins."

Vian was in the kitchen telling a friend on the phone about the fight.

Jan shouted to her again, "Bring me a piece of ice."

Vian held a tray with a mug containing ice cubes in her hands as she spoke on the phone, balancing it between her tilted head and shoulder, then returned to the kitchen. Jan placed an ice cube on his forehead and kept it until half melted and dripped into the tray.

He shouted to Vian for the third time, "Everyone is congratulating me on beating the official, but they ask for the clip of the beating. It doesn't satisfy their appetite that I broke the guard's back, but they're interested in the official's testicles. Should we go to tell him that we love to cancel our agreement and he's free to do whatever he loves?"

Vian didn't answer. Jan placed another piece of ice on his forehead.

"Damn. She's busy promoting the film," he said, then smiled at the idea with his eyebrows furrowing at the cold ice. "But this's better. One of Vian's friends will publish the full film for the public, as her son correctly said for the first time in his life. Or, as Vian more correctly put it, all her friends will, except the envious ones. I'm dying to see the reaction of that feminist who destroyed my nerves by hitting her notebook with the tip of the pen. As for that guard; that scoundrel brought back the nightmare for the second time. I should've added the activist's share of the beating and broken another table with his back."

He continued to cure his forehead with the ice while Vian continued publishing the video. He called out to her to get more pieces of ice. Jan began a new course of treatment that he didn't believe would work.

Tara walked in.

"What are you doing?" she asked him.

"Did you have amnesia?" he asked. "This's the fourth time to ask this question."

"It's the third time," she said.

"You know how many times you have asked and yet you don't get tired of repeating the question," he said. "Next time, send Milo to do the job of annoying me instead of you. At least I can kick it on its ugly ass."

"You didn't answer me," she said. "What are you doing?"

"This's what one can rationally call irrational urge," he said. "I told you I hit two huge people, then one of them managed to scratch my head with his dirty hand and make it allergic."

"The last time you said the man took advantage of your inattention and scratched your head against the table, and the time before that you said—"

"Okay, enough of that," he interrupted her. "What exactly do you want me to say?"

"Say that he bothered you and that you cried and hit your head with the table," she replied.

"Huh?"

"Come on, say it," she said.

"Have you come recently from Mars?" he asked. "All the inhabitants on this planet congratulated me for beating the two men and are asking for more, and you want me to be the one who was beaten."

"I want to see the sheep come home," she said.

"Uh, I see," he said, throwing the rest of the ice cubes into the tray. "You want me to go back to my old character. The loser who hits his head against the wall if he doesn't like something and then cries like a child."

"No. He cries like a child and then hits his head against the wall. Go back to your old *karatker*, Dad," she said.

"To play with you?"

"Yes."

"So, you're dreaming," he said. "Your old father died. Didn't you go to visit his grave with Milo? If you didn't, we all three will go to put on his grave a dry rose that we'll take from a garbage can in a flower shop. Or we snatch grass from the mouth of a sheep you like for your father's grave."

Vian entered the room merrily.

"I sent the two clips to dozens of friends, pages, and groups," she said.

"Well done," he said. "There's someone here who wants to post the clip of the bodyguard hitting, I mean scratching my head with the table, or with his hand, or with his testicles."

"That won't happen," Vian said, and then turned to Tara, waggling her index finger. "Go to Milo, he's calling you."

Tara walked away and then looked over her shoulder.

"I'll be back later," she said. "Our account is not over."

Jan stuck out his tongue to her. Tara entered her room and closed the door.

"She's the one most negatively affected by the wolf bite," Jan said. "Come on, let me see the clip on your account and the reactions. Your daughter almost poisoned my soul."

Jan spent two glorious hours reading the comments and rewatching the two clips of the fight.

"I think it's time for me to cut short my vacation and go back to work," he said after he finished and felt satisfied.

"They'll roll you out the red carpet," she said.

"Or they'll hide from fear," he said.

"Don't let anything happen without filming it," she said.

"Of course, unless ten people gather around me and give me salty and sour kicks," he said.

"Ten people wouldn't get together to fight at work," she said. "They usually gather at parties."

"Right," he said. "Hundreds at a party and thousands in the city and outside for Nawroz, but you see a few employees protesting against their manager or the government. I think I should regret attempting to celebrate the seventeenth of February."

Jan called his boss at night about abbreviating his vacation. His boss told him what Vian had expected: he was welcome whenever he returned.

News broke at his workplace before he arrived there the next morning. The reception staff greeted him with genuine enthusiasm. They recounted the quarrel to him as if he hadn't been there.

The director's close staff sat in his office while others stood, all waiting for Jan. With a smile on his face, the director got up from his desk and headed toward him.

Jan was scratching his forehead from time to time and cursing the bodyguard in secret.

The director asked him to submit a request to return to work. He promised to mediate with someone more influential than the official whom Jan had beaten to expedite the administrative process beyond the usual timeframe.

Jan walked out of the director's room with the previous scene repeating in the rest of the workplace. He then went to his workroom with his colleagues who repeated every comment he had already heard. As his excitement continued, his forehead began to throb. He felt the need to wash it off with cold water.

"Will you allow me to go to the toilet for two minutes?" Jan asked his male and female colleagues. "I was so happy to be back with you that I forgot to urinate at home."

All laughed.

Jan hurried to leave the room.

"Better to express your need to urinate and then do it while they watch than to tell them the story of the head and the table," he said to himself.

The workday ended with the manager reassuring Jan that he would send the official letter tomorrow and with Jan being upset about his forehead itching. It bothered him more when it hindered him from imposing his new personality and harassing two employees he hated.

At home, Vian asked him for details of the visit. He had none except the warm welcome with which he was received, but without the red carpet or quarreling with anyone. Then he remembered his fake need to urinate and told her the story.

Jan waited a few days until the official approval to end his vacation arrived. He spent those days reading what people had written about the hotel fight and their reactions and comments. He felt he had become a hero who needed new exploits. Good luck patted him again when his forehead itching subsided, letting him enjoy the new situation.

To erase his shameful old history in front of his intrusive neighbor, he constantly went out into the garden and climbed on the tree on which Vian used to climb during her strange fits. Every time his neighbor came to his garden, Jan shook the tree violently, then got down from it, then went up to it, shook it again, and repeated this to make his neighbor ask him about his wolf condition. The neighbor bothered him for two days by not asking him anything, satisfied by just watching him.

This damn neighbor envies me and doesn't want me to express myself in front of him, he said to himself. *Or maybe he's afraid of me. Come on, you fat bald. Don't be afraid, I won't bite you in obedience to religious orders regarding the consideration of neighbors, even if dumber than you.*

But the neighbor remained silent until the third day when he noticed Jan at the top of the tree for the tenth time. The man placed his forearms on the wall separating the two houses.

"It seems that Madam Vian no longer has the desire to climb trees," he said.

"Is that all you care about?" Jan asked him.

"Of course not," the man replied. "I also care about your safety. Be careful not to fall."

"Did you ever see lions fall from trees?" Jan asked.

"No, but I saw men falling from it," the man replied.

"And you also didn't see monkeys falling from trees," Jan said.

"Of course not," the neighbor replied.

"Then come up here and don't be afraid."

The man understood Jan's hint, but he didn't answer and returned to watching him. Then he went back inside. Jan came down from the tree and at a height of less than a meter from the ground, he jumped down. The jump was uncalculated and Jan fell to his face, hitting his forehead with the ground.

"Oh, no. Not my forehead again," he shouted.

He sat on the grass, stretching his legs apart like a child. He tapped his forehead with the right forefinger twice.

"It wasn't a hard blow, but the memories it brought back were bitter," he said. "Thank God my neighbor was gone before he saw me fall like a kid."

Chapter 13

The Return of the Lamb

On the fourth day, Jan woke up and saw the clock at nine. He jumped out of bed.

"I told her to wake me up before going to work," he said. "And of course, the breakfast is as cold as a fridge. It's as self-evident as a triangle has three angles."

He opened his mouth to growl. He couldn't. He gathered his breath to express his anger.

"Didn't I tell you that I don't want to hear the alarm and I want you to..." his voice came out sharp, his eyes wide open.

He put his hand over his mouth.

"No, not this," he said.

Then he collapsed, sitting on the bed.

Tara heard his voice and ran to his bedroom.

"I heard something," she told him.

"What did you hear?" he asked in a low voice.

"I heard a man screaming like a crying baby," she replied.

"Who else is in the house?" he asked, again in a low voice, his hand still over his mouth.

"Dana went to school and Mom to work and I'm in the afternoon session, Milo is asleep and you're the only one awake," she answered. "Who screamed like a crying baby?"

"Nobody," Jan answered, then furrowed his eyebrows and pretended to be anxious.

"Maybe a neighbor's child came in," he said, trying to make his voice rough. "Let's search the house and arrest that child on charges of trespassing on other people's property."

His attempt couldn't dupe Tara as she could perceive the sharpness of his voice. She approached him and sat on the bed beside him.

"Open your mouth," she said.

"I feel a burning sensation in my throat," he said. "Stay away, it could be the flu."

"You're not sick. Open your eyes."

She looked into his eyes. They were shaking.

"They look like sheep's eyes," she said. "Where are the wolf's gazes?"

Then she jumped from the bed to the floor and bounced in place.

"My father is back to his old self!" she yelled with uncontrolled joy.

Jan ran toward her and put his hand over her mouth.

"Be quiet, the neighbors will hear us," he said in a hoarse voice.

She evaded him, ran to the bed, climbed onto it, and bounced on top of it.

"The lamb has returned to our house! The lamb has returned to our house!" she yelled.

Grabbing her from under her armpits, he got her off the bed. Frowning, he put his hand over her mouth and pressed it.

"Now you are the one who will be arrested, but on charges of endangering wolfish security," he told her.

She raised her head to him and looked into his eyes with laughing eyes. With a face full of joy, she removed his hand from her mouth.

"Lamb's eyes! Lamb's eyes!" she shouted.

He covered her eyes with his hand.

She clasped her hands behind her back. "Did you play hide and seek like this when you were a kid?" she asked.

Dumbfounded and not knowing what to do, he remained silent for a while. Then suddenly he snapped his thumb and middle finger.

"Yes, hide and seek!" he exclaimed happily. "That's what we're going to do."

He quickly changed his clothes, grabbed Tara's hand, and dragged her out. Tara walked with him, pulling herself back.

"The children of the past were weird," she said.

Jan opened the passenger's door, put his hands under her armpits, and took her in. He closed the door, turned to the driver's seat, got in, and slammed the door shut.

Unable to say anything useful to prevent the impending damage, he drove without the intention of speaking. Tara was leaning back on her seat, her arms crossed over her chest. The car headed out of town. Tara knew the destination. She turned to him, still crossing her arms.

"Are we going to play hide and seek in our farm?" she asked.

Jan didn't answer her as his mind was preoccupied with how to hide his return to his old state from others, especially his wife.

"The first thing is to get this creature to shut up," he said, turning his head to Tara. "And this creature won't shut up, just as a triangle won't have four angles."

When at the farm, Jan got down and opened the chain-link fence. He got into the car, took it into the garage, got out again, and closed the fence.

Still silent, he unlocked the outer door of the house and pushed Tara inside. He locked the door and put the key in his pocket.

"When are we going to play?" Tara asked him.

"We're not going to play," he replied, pushing her slightly to sit on a chair. "We'll stay here until I make sure you don't tell your mother that I was back to my old self. Did I tell you I'm kidnapping you?"

"No, you didn't," she answered, swinging her legs hanging off the chair. "You said something else I don't know what it means."

Then she jumped from the chair and stood up. "Let's go home," she said, grabbing his hand with hers and pulling it.

Her father pushed her back to sit on the chair. "I'm not going to bring you home until you give me guarantees that you won't speak," he told her.

She turned her face to one side as if she wanted to hear well. "Give you what?" she asked.

"Guarantees," he replied.

Then he mocked himself, "Guarantees! Hah! Guarantees from a child! The sheep is unrealistic even in its terminology."

But he had to take guarantees, something important, anyway.

"I'm going to withhold something that belongs to you," he said to her. "It won't be your dirty dog, Milo, because I'll have to live with it until my demands are fully met. No, it's your favorite doll, silly Doodoo. And if you speak, I'll execute him and separate his head from his body."

"Then you'll buy me another one, right?" Tara asked him.

"Wrong," he answered. "And therefore you insist on talking. You're going to force me to kidnap Milo."

"That's fine if we stay here. I'll play with him," she said as she swung her legs again.

Jan didn't know how to answer. He stayed standing in the room for a while, then crossed his hands behind his back and began pacing the room nervously.

"Negotiating with this child is harder than negotiating with the nuclear president of North Korea," he said.

After completing three turns, he stopped in the middle of the room.

"The problem is that I have no negotiating cards other than the threat to execute Doodoo, which is like the threat to spit in the sea."

He resumed pacing the room while Tara looked at him. There was no explanation for his return to his old state other than the blows his forehead received on the table at that party, or his falling on his face in the garden, or both.

"It's the silliest thing in history," he said, moving closer to the wall and thinking to hit it with his forehead. "You need a wolf to bite you to turn into a wolf, but just for a dog to hit your head with a table or fall from a height of one meter to lose your wolfish self. It's really a fake wolfness."

He stopped in front of the wall and didn't turn around.

"And who knows, maybe it wasn't a pack of wolves, but just a failed gang of stray dogs. I've never heard of wolves in that area in my life, as Vian said and I didn't believe her," he said, then glued his forehead and nose to the wall.

"My only consolation is that I picked up that human dog and slammed him against the table in front of people," he said, turning then around. "Maybe that ninety-kilogram lift of that sack of shit was the reason my wolf's batteries were so quickly discharged."

Reaching the dead end of his analysis, he resumed moving across the room with his hands behind his back, then switched to moving in circles. Tara kept watching him and swinging her legs.

** ** **

Jan and Tara remained missing until night. Jan's phone was switched off. Vian called for the hundredth time. While Jan's phone was ringing, she moved her phone away from her ear.

"Something happened to them," she said to Dana, and then put the phone on the table. Dana shrugged.

"That's better," he said. "We got rid of two annoying people. We'll be living in peace for the rest of our lives. I don't mind if you want to get married. You're still young and a lot of men would covet your wealth."

Vian showed her displeasure with the facial expressions the family used to see: she closed her mouth with a shadow of a smile and looked at Dana through a narrow slit of her eyes.

"Excuse me?" she asked.

"And of course for your beauty above all."

Vian closed her eyes completely, picking up then the phone to try another call. Dana turned around, walked over to the sofa, jumped on it, and lay down, bouncing.

"If my father doesn't answer until tomorrow, let the family know that you're open to marriage proposals," he said, then he took a final leap and sat upright.

"I'll spread the news to everyone I know," he said, bouncing again, slowly.

"It's either Jan or nobody," she said.

Dana stopped bouncing. "I understand this for the old Jan who was crying like a child in front of you," he said, "But the transformed Jan who growls like a dog—"

"Hold your tongue," she interrupted as she pulled the phone away from her ear. "Say like a lion. Like a tiger."

"Okay. I admit I don't understand women."

"What about Tara?" she asked. "Will I adopt a girl instead of her?"

"It's a worse idea than my father coming back," he replied.

Jan's phone was still switched off. It became worrying. Vian called the police who told her to stop by the station the next day. She insisted on them and they told her to pass by the guard officer. She took Dana with her and ordered him not to say a word. They entered the police station.

"Who kidnapped whom?" asked the duty officer sitting at his desk as he looked at his papers and flipped them through with annoyance he didn't try to hide.

"My husband kidnapped my daughter," she replied.

"Ha! The usual story," said the officer without taking his head off the papers. "Wives deprive husbands of their children and then accuse them of kidnapping them."

Vian's eyes narrowed and she smiled wryly.

"Are you misogynistic?" she asked quietly.

Ignoring her question, the officer raised his head to her, gathered the papers into one stack, and then slammed the edge of the stack on the table to straighten it out.

"We take information from you and then call you when we get to a conclusion," he said.

When they left the station, Vian and Dana agreed that the misogynistic officer would not do his duty with enthusiasm.

"Consider we didn't come here," Vian said to her son when heading toward her car. "I'll use my means to find them."

"Why did you tell the officer that your husband kidnapped your daughter?" Dana asked her. "Aren't you afraid they'll take him to prison?"

"I'm not going to belittle Jan and tell people that an ordinary person kidnapped the wolf," she replied.

"I'm pulling out my question," Dana said. "I should've expected this from you with a wolf in our house. If he actually kidnapped her, you should know why."

"You can't predict what a wolf will do," she said.

She stopped and smiled, then looked at the dark horizon.

"You wild wolf," she said as if speaking to herself. "You want to control me more and have me fall at your feet?"

Then she shrugged. "So what? Oh, how I love that, you savage."

**   **   **

At his house on the farm, Jan was still pacing back and forth across the room with his hands behind his back until he felt dizzy. Tara was turning her head as he moved left and right.

"How's your throat?" she asked him.

"What about it?"

"Didn't you say it hurt?"

Jan halted in the corner of the room.

"Stop your psychological warfare against me," he said. "You know my throat works as vigorously as the drum of a concrete mixer truck. Simply, I was back to my old self."

He approached her, pulled her braid up, and shook her head.

"You only care about seeing your father as a child crying," he said. "But you don't care about what your father wants."

He stopped shaking her head and kept holding her braid. Tara nodded, moving her father's hand up and down.

"And you only care about growing up," she said, then stopped nodding.

"What's your problem?" he asked and returned to bobbing her head up and down.

"We have no child in our home except me," she answered.

Tara had told her father dozens of times she saw him as a child a little older than her.

"Don't I have the right to grow up?" he asked.

"We grow up together," she said.

"Believe me, your mother is also a big baby," he said. "Play with her."

"She's an annoying kid," she said. "She doesn't cry like a baby when something bothers her. She just half-shuts her eyes and smiles like you're a cockroach."

"Okay. When you turn thirty years old, I'll be an old cockroach of eighty years old and I'll say to you, "Choo you allo me choo gro up?'"

"When I turn thirty, you'll be seventy years old."

"Sixty-two years, you oppressor."

She grabbed his hand and dragged it to her. "It doesn't matter. Let's go home and play."

Jan freed his hand from her, put his hand behind his back, and returned to the room back and forth. He stopped after two rounds and switched to motion on the diagonal of the room.

"Maybe this direction matches the Earth's magnetic field and eliminates my mental confusion," he said.

Tara continued to move her head along with her father's nervous movement in the room.

"Let's go home and play there, you stubborn kid," she said.

"We can play here," he said.

Tara repeated her request and Jan repeated his offer. They changed the topic, then changed it again, and continued moving from one topic to another. Jan's mind was busy finding a solution to his problem while Tara kept disturbing his thoughts. He stopped suddenly and turned to her.

"Listen," he said. "I can make a deal with you."

Tara put her index fingers in her ears.

"I won't listen if it's not for you playing with me," she said.

"It'll be in our deal," he said.

She pulled her fingers out of her ears.

"Then I'll listen," she said.

"This's our agreement," Jan said. "Don't mention to anyone that I have returned to my old, silly self. When others are with us, you act with me as if I were a wolf. And when we're alone, I act with you as if I were a cat, a dog, a worm. Whatever you want."

It seemed to Tara a reasonable offer. She grabbed her chin with two fingers.

"Hmm. Let me think of it," she said.

Chapter 14

Fears of the Former Wolf

The family reunited before noon the next day. Jan waited for his wife's inquiries, but the day passed without questions and answers. This eased his anxiety a little although he knew his wife would start an interrogation suddenly and without warning. Contrary to his expectation, this didn't happen until night.

The bell rang at night. Jan jerked. And when Vian went to open the door, he feared they were guests coming to inquire about the incident.

Vian came back alone carrying a parcel. It didn't surprise Jan. His wife seemed to be practicing her strange nature. He even expected the parcel to contain firecrackers and fireworks she would launch from the roof of the house to celebrate his and Tara's return.

He waited for her to open the parcel to avoid asking her about its contents in his pre-wolfish era voice. Vian didn't stop in the room and went with the parcel to the guest room.

Jan resisted his urge to follow her and find out what he discovered half an hour later. It was a small party Vian arranged for the four of them: a large cake with one burning candle and no crackers or fireworks.

Jan's struggle to deepen his voice prevented him from talking much. His intuition about the party being a celebration of his and Tara's safe return proved true. The cake explained its presence, but Jan wished Vian would reveal the mystery of the unexplainable single candle, herself. Two candles meant him and Tara. One meant him alone, and this he couldn't believe. If that had been the time of his wolfness, he would have thought so conclusively, even if Vian had said the candle wasn't for him.

Woe for my wolfness' short era, he bemoaned himself, *I was so confident in myself that if Vian had put two candles on the cake for me and Tara, I would've pulled out Tara's candle, chewed it, and then spit it out in the toilets.*

In the end, he decided to kick that glorious history out of his head because it kept belittling his recent self. He remained silent for a few minutes, waiting for an explanation from Vian.

Nothing. Then another nothing. Then it was time he couldn't bear keeping the question in his mind and getting nothing. He gathered the scattered pieces of his courage.

Pointing with his waggling index finger at the cake, he said two words in a hoarse voice, "One candle."

Adding "and a big cake" was a risky extravagance in speech.

Smiling, Vian leaned over the table, made a ring with her mouth, waited for a few seconds, and then blew out the candle.

"Of course, it has to be one," she replied to her husband's remark while still bent over the cake, adding more ambiguity to the already ambiguous situation. She then proceeded to cut the cake with graceful movements, smiling and turning sideways toward Jan. Jan wished he hadn't asked her. He risked talking to then get another nothing in return.

Welcome back to the era of failed projects, dude, he thought to himself. *Next time, make an economic feasibility before you speak.*

Jan spent the next few minutes silently eating his share of the cake. With the plate lifted to his mouth, he was chewing and looking at the family from right to left as if he had committed a crime and was afraid to be exposed. He waited for someone to volunteer and explain the mystery of the candle. His mind was so preoccupied with what was coming next he didn't notice the cake crumbs falling from his mouth onto the plate. Then he realized that his continued silence would raise doubts about his wolfness.

His brain was rotating like a mill to find something to say while his jaws were chewing the cake over and over again until it turned into water in his mouth.

Then he forgot about the candle and began to speak, choosing the fewest words he needed. Trying to raise topics safely, he posed short questions that would elicit long answers. It didn't work. The answers were shorter than his questions:

"What's our program for the coming days?" Jan asked, chewing, and with the plate near his mouth.

"The usual program," replied Vian.

He looked at Dana. "Did Dana prepare for midterm exams?" he asked as if he were talking about someone else.

"No, Dana didn't prepare," Dana replied.

Jan wanted to ask Tara a question but was afraid of her. Tara's eyes radiated as she ate from her plate near her mouth like him, but smiling.

"Who asked about me during my absence?" he asked, instead.

"Nobody," Dana replied.

"Yes, your brother," Vian corrected Dana.

"Oh, right," Dana said. "And our neighbor."

"The bald on the right?" Jan asked with the intrusive neighbor in his mind.

"No," Dana replied. "The bald on the left."

"And Milo," said Tara.

Liar, Jan thought. *Yes, liar and exploitative and unscrupulous. We were together without your filthy dog. When did you see it to hear it asking about me?*

Jan's short questions and answers continued for an additional two minutes, which amounted to two hours.

It's not their fault, he thought to himself. *It's my ridiculous questions and topics that if anyone kindly participates with me, it would be out of great decency or to help the afflicted.*

During those failed attempts and when he was silent, Jan acted like a wolf for seconds, his heart trembling with fear, though. His eyes were on his daughter, who ate with a full mouth and winked at him now and then to reassure him that she was still committed to the agreement.

Noticing Vian smiling incessantly made him guess that his acting hadn't deceived her and those smiles were mocking him. This was harder for him than his daughter having a powerful weapon against him. He wished Vian would confront him with her thoughts. Waiting to be alone with her was his only choice to make her say it openly and save him from the torment of anticipation.

Dana was the first to leave the party, licking his lips from the remnants of the cake with a mocking expression on his face. Jan loved to scold him for that as his son used to mock parties more important and reasonable parties than this one. It was an opportunity to forget his fears about exposing the loss of his wolfness.

"You didn't like it, huh?" Jan asked him, continuing to economize on words.

"What didn't I like?" Dana asked.

Damn! Jan said to himself. *He lures me to talk more than I want.*

Then he answered in a hoarse voice, "The party."

He felt relieved he only needed two words and Dana would be the one to speak now.

Dana disappointed him when he replied with a question that needed an answer, "Why wouldn't I like it?"

I'm sorry, son of a dog, Jan said to himself. *I was wrong when I spoke to you. Consider me inferior to Milo if I ask you anything from now on.*

Jan decided the attempt to scold Dana had failed and the conversation should end here. He made a ring with his lips, tilted his head to the side, and raised it toward the ceiling as if thinking.

Tara got up and followed her brother. With his tilted head still raised toward the ceiling, Jan looked down at her to be sure she would keep their secret until the last moment.

Before walking out the door, Tara turned over her shoulder and winked at him. Jan gazed at her, marveling at how she, a mere child, possessed a stronger character than he did.

With his neck still cocked upward, his eyes shifted from his daughter to the ceiling.

I feel the need to cry for myself, he said to himself. *But I have to postpone it. I'll cry when I'm alone. Yes, I swear I'll cry a lot.*

He straightened his neck, which began to hurt him, and turned to Vian, who remained alone with him. She was smiling. This almost destroyed his nerves. Jan picked the words to be as few as possible. He recalled the year when he started learning Spanish. When speaking with a Mexican engineer, he considered every sentence before saying it.

Having such a shaking memory, I know now that becoming a torero and wrestling with a Mexican toro was easier than learning the Mexican man's language, he thought to himself. *At least I could learn how to deal with this family that possesses a strong personality. Three bulls against one sheep. No, that's not fair. Or, as the bull shouted in the loudspeaker, 'Eso no es justo. Todos estos toreros en mi contra,' but the audience didn't listen and encouraged him to accept his death like a man.*

He gathered his courage to start playing the role of a wolf.

"Look," he said to Vian, trying to roughen his voice again. "I kidnapped Tara for something important. I won't mention it. So I'm warning you not to—"

"I know," she interrupted him with a smile.

He swallowed. "You know?" he asked her.

"Mm," she said, still smiling.

Jan cleared his throat to make sure his voice came out raspy. "Ahem. Did that creature tell you anything?" he asked, moving his thumb toward the door Tara went out from.

Vian approached him, put her elbow on his shoulder, and gently stroked his chin with her index finger.

"She said nothing," she replied. "And what kind of important things does she have to say?" then she poked his chin again.

"Okay, that's enough," Jan said. "Ahem. We're not at Doctor Nasreen's."

"Yes, enough talk, let's continue our celebration of your return," she said, poking his chin again.

"It's also enough to hit my chin with your finger. Ahem," he said. "You women are fond of nerve-wracking little strokes. Has anyone else said anything to you? Ahem."

"I don't need anyone to tell me that the wolf wanted to do something violent to remind us that he was still a wolf."

"Hah?" Jan said, gaping.

"Yes, you wolf," she said, holding his chin with two fingers of her hand that rested on his shoulder. "I should expect other moves from you."

He saw the looks of admiration in her eyes while his mouth was still open in astonishment.

Vian turned around, walked toward the sofa, and sat on it. She stuck her legs together, wrapped her hands around her knees, and looked at him with a smile. Jan was stunned for a few seconds and then he understood.

Yes, yes! he said to himself. *Tara has kept her gentleman's promise. How great you are, my exploitative, criminal daughter!*

He tightened his posture and fixed his eyes on his wife with a gaze he wanted could be as hard as reinforcement steel bars.

"Yes, right," he said in a voice he wanted could be of harder steel bars. "I must remind you all from time to time. I've seen you becoming accustomed to my wolfness."

He noticed that he spoke without thinking about the economy of words. Vian got up to leave the room.

"Where to?" he roared disapprovingly. "I'm not finished yet."

"I know," she said. "I'll make coffee for you and me and then sit down together to sip it while you continue talking. Or would you like me to bring you tea?"

He wanted to order a citrus cocktail he used to prepare for himself to strengthen his immunity, but his load of artificial wolfness was almost over. Coffee and tea were easier to mention than a list of fruits.

"Ahem. Yes, coffee. Or tea. Or anything. Ahem. Okay, coffee."

Vian went to the kitchen. Before she left the room, Jan recalled the story of the lonely candle.

"One candle, huh?" he asked in a rough voice, almost sure now of her answer.

"Yes, one candle," she answered, nodding twice coquettishly and without turning around. "For the wolf who roams alone in the forests in search of his she-wolf."

Jan stayed alone in front of the couch. The effort he put into playing the wolf was too much for him. He exhaled so hard that he thought he was about to burn the room down.

"She did well by going," he said. "I only had those sentences. Maybe I was repeating them: I didn't finish, I didn't finish, yes coffee, yes tea. And then the mask of the lone, fake wolf who fears the forests would fall and he'd head to the wall and butt it with his head."

The stress of the situation on his nerves made him collapse on a couch he thought was behind him. He fell on his butt on the floor. His lips pressed together to stifle a painful cry.

"It's a big responsibility to be a wolf," he said, his voice cracking with pain. "The life of a sheep is easier until they slaughter it."

He buckled at the sides.

"If a person falls a thousand times on his butt, he won't turn into a wolf puppy," he said. "Why didn't Vian put a sofa here too for such sheepy moments like this?"

Chapter 15

The Confession

Jan made an extraordinary effort to create the wolf character at home while maintaining the economy of speech. The task was easier at his workplace since his colleagues had seen him in his wolfish state only once.

His agreement with Tara required extra exertion. He had to keep up with her in her affairs, especially playing with her and her dog. At first, they played when alone. Then Tara's demands increased. She began to lock the room and play with her father when Vian and Dana were at home. Her excuse was to study lessons without anyone disturbing them.

Then the job began to press on Jan's nerves and muscles. His requests for breaks were of no avail. Each session ended with his collapse and lying on his back on the floor and recalling the glory of his lost wolfish period.

In the final days of enduring the task, Tara asked him to imitate a cat. It wasn't the first time, but her current demand was to imitate the cat in a way that would make Milo chase him. Jan rebelled.

"Okay, listen," he said to her. "I can imitate the sounds of cats, dogs, and frogs. But I've never been a dog to know why dogs love to chase cats."

"Just imitate the cat and Milo will chase you," Tara said. "He's smart, believe me."

"No, Milo is stupid and I don't believe anything you say. I imitated ten cats, two male cats, and one transgender but stupid Milo chased none of them."

She patted him on the cheek. "Listen to my words and don't let Mama hear us," she said.

Jan obeyed her veiled threat while muttering to himself his disapproval of her vile blackmail of him. He knelt on his hands and knees and began to meow in the face of Milo who didn't respond. Then he turned around and looked over his shoulder at the dog and meowed. Milo remained seated on its hind legs, looking once at Jan and another at Tara. Then it barked at Jan.

Jan snarled, "Come on chase me, you dirty dog. If I had known that you were worth something, I would've made you bite me to turn me back into a wolf, but I know I would turn into a mean puppy. Chase me, you who have no value, nor Marxist surplus value, nor capitalist added value. Come on, son of a dog!"

"Don't talk like that to Milo, Dad," Tara said. "He understands you."

"If this jackass understands anything, it would chase me," Jan said. "What do you think, should I imitate a rat?"

"No, keep imitating the cat."

The scene lasted a long time. Jan changed his position several times in vain until his nerves finally collapsed and he fell on his stomach, sprawling on the floor.

"Come on, Dad," Tara whispered, pretending to speak without letting her mother hear. "Do your job before my mother knocks on the door."

Jan remained lying on his stomach, his right cheek glued to the floor. Milo barked at him from the other side. Jan turned his head to the left, pressed his cheek to the floor, and spat at the dog. Milo answered with a short bark. Jan got up to his feet and dusted his hands.

"Are you convinced?" Tara asked.

"Yes, but to do what everyone with dignity should do in these circumstances," Jan replied. "I announce from this musty-smelling room that the film has ended with the failure of the comedian and his dismissal from work without pay. Then the director going back home in a taxi and giving the Oscar to the taxi driver to throw it into the nearest sewer. And finally, the car falling into the sewer and the sewer lid entering the driver's throat."

He headed toward the door.

"What are you doing?" Tara asked.

"I'm going to confess everything to your mother. It's better to endure the contempt of the lady of the house than the house dog despising me."

He opened the door, walked out, and slammed it shut. Tara looked at her dog.

"Do you think he can do that?" she asked.

Milo cocked his head to the side.

"You also don't know?" asked Tara.

When Jan left the room, Vian saw him red-faced. Crossing one leg over the other on the sofa, she was filing her nails.

"It looks like you were studying beet farming," she said as she looked at him, then went back to her work.

"Red or white?" asked Jan.

"What's red or white?" Vian asked.

"Beets," answered Jan.

She looked at him.

"It was red and now it's white," she said.

"Look, I want to confess to you," he said.

"About what? Whether the beets in your lesson were red or white?"

"Damn all the beets of the world in all their colors," he replied. "No, I want to confess to you about my damned wolfness."

"Don't call it damned," she said. "It's great."

"Great or inferior. A wolf bit me one day and it's all over."

"Oh, honey, I understand you," she said, placing the nail file on the table and uncrossing her leg. "You have been attacked by nostalgia for your wolf brothers. Maybe you also want to bite them and have them bite you."

"No, screw it again, not that. Where do I get a pack of wolves attacking me and then the least polite and ethical of them pounce on me and bite me and then... and then..."

"And then what?"

"And then..."

"Then what, my dear?"

Jan fell on his butt in the middle of the room. He laughed a little, then cried a little with joy, and then giggled.

"How clever you are, my wonderful wife!" he exclaimed. "Yes. Yes. I long for another bite to renew the wolfish blood running in my veins."

Still sitting on the floor, he stretched out his hands forward and parted his tense fingers. He knew he did well not cutting his nails.

"Awooo. Awooo," he imitated the sound of wolves howling.

Tara walked out of her room.

"You're scaring Milo, you fierce wolf," she said and then winked at him.

"Go back to your room," he ordered her. "And don't let the dog that's afraid to chase fake cats come out, because I'm having a wolfish fit."

Then he added in a low voice. "Get out of my face, you unscrupulous liar, exploitative actress, and don't forget to tell Milo that your father still thinks it's a dirty dog."

Jan and Vian agreed to visit the place near the airport fence where the wolves attacked them. Vian suggested they be there at exactly twelve o'clock at night. Jan agreed without asking about the reason for this "exactly." He was never interested in the myths related to wolves. All he wanted was one bite from one wolf at any time of the day. A bite, even from a wolf puppy. He was ready to bow down to that wolf pup and kiss its foot for just one bite.

The moon was in the middle of the sky and close to full but neither of them noticed it.

When they arrived at the scene, Jan knelt and lit a fire. Vian knelt beside him, put her hand on his shoulder, and smiled.

"Aren't you going to say, like last time, that the airport guards will see the fire and come arrest us?" she asked.

Jan stretched his tense fingers to his mouth and bared his teeth.

"Let them come and I'll tear them apart with my fangs. Grrrr."

The two sat on the ground side by side, waiting for the wolves to come until the fire almost died out. Jan got up and brought herbs and small twigs and threw them into the fire. Then Vian went and brought other herbs. No one came for an hour. Jan re-lit the fire more than once. He wrapped his arms around his knees.

"I'm afraid that the security forces will come and one of them will bite me and turn me into a volunteer policeman without pay," he said.

"If they come, I'll bite them and turn them into security women without maternity leave," Vian said.

Another hour passed without any wolf or human coming. Jan's patience was running out.

"Regarding the wolf bite, I'm one hundred percent sure it was true," he said. "But don't you think that the arrival of the security men last time was not a dream? Why didn't they come now?"

"It wasn't a dream," she answered. "You know that a lot of our government's stuff is moody and what it applies now it forgets tomorrow. It resembles me in my strange matters."

"But it's a ridiculous government, unlike you, dear Vivi. Grrrr."

Vian rose to her feet and dusted off her butt.

"Let's go home," she said. "You don't need your brother wolves. They need you. If they want to see you, let them send a message asking for an appointment."

Jan got up. As his wife expected, he didn't go to the car, but moved away from her and began collecting herbs and twigs again. He returned and threw them into the faint fire. He knelt, pressed his face to the ground, and blew on the fire.

"We're not going anywhere until I confess to you," he said without looking up at her, then he blew.

"Confess to what?" Vian asked, "That you lost your wolfness?"

Her question fell on Jan's head like a thunderbolt. He stayed for a while bending over and staring at the ground with his nose close to it. Then he turned his head to his wife.

"You knew or you concluded?" he asked.

"It doesn't make any difference. I concluded."

"Since when?"

"Since Tara and you started closing the door. I heard you obey Tara like a slave in everything she asked of you. I heard you complaining. I heard her reminding you of an agreement between you. And I heard you meowing like cats, crowing like roosters, and clucking like chickens."

"And did you hear me bark at Milo like a puppy so Tara would keep my secret?"

"So much and I heard you braying like a donk... well. I concluded that Tara was riding on your back and leading you around the room."

"And you kept silent and didn't grieve for the loss of the wolf you adored and for my transformation from a wolf into a donkey?"

"I pretended not to know," she answered. "I imagined it never happened. My consolation was that everyone saw you as a wolf and no one knew you were back to your old self. And we won't let anyone know."

Jan rose to his feet.

"Then, after this mutual confession, you'll no longer be able to play the role of the one who doesn't know, and I won't be able to play the role of the wolf who knows that he is fake. I'm sorry that I disappointed you. I'm ready to go to the zoo and enter the wolf's cage for you. And if the wolf considers me too despicable to attack, I'll keep harassing him until he bites me."

She grabbed his arm and gently pulled him toward the car.

"Let's go home and decide later whether a zoo wolf bites you or I should do," she said.

"Tell you something? I'll ask Tara to play with me in the living room. There's no need for her messy room that looks like the vomit of a herd of dinosaurs."

"No. Not in the living room, not in her room, or anywhere else," she said. "Since I knew the truth, your agreement with Tara has fallen through."

"She'll blackmail us by telling others that her father has become a sheep again."

"No one will believe a child."

"That unscrupulous girl won't accept her defeat," he said.

"Don't worry, I'll support you in your fight with her," she said.

"Do you think we're going to make it? She's a fierce fighter."

"We will win. We're two to one."

Vian got him into the passenger seat and turned around the car toward the driver's seat. She opened the door and put a leg in the car, half sitting on the seat, with her left hand holding the door handle from the inside. She looked at the moon that dangled toward the horizon to set. Closing her eyes halfway, she smiled and slowly shook her head left and right.

"Oh, you, the great night that brought the wolves here," she said as if in a dream. "You only happen once in a lifetime."

Chapter 16

Husbands and Wives

Jan and Vian returned at dawn. Vian opened the gate, moved ahead of Jan through the yard, and unlocked the inner door. Carelessly, she entered the hallway and then the living room. Jan followed her, walking on his tiptoes.

Vian turned to him. "What's wrong?" she asked.

Jan put his finger over his mouth. "Hush!" he said in a low voice. "Let the little dragon sleep. Any discussion with her means depriving me of sleep."

Vian smiled and walked back to him, grabbed his arm, and gently pulled him toward their bedroom.

"Don't be so afraid of her," she said. "If she gets out of her room, I'll send her back to it."

"Okay, let's go into our room and lock the door with the key. That's safer."

Fortunately for Jan, nothing disturbed his sleep that night, and then he enjoyed a morning when Tara slept until ten. However, vacationing and staying at home meant more chances to face Dana with the new situation and let Tara know that her mother had learned about that situation. The bright side of the weekend was he had time to practice false wolfness before going back to work.

The day started as usual at the breakfast table. Tara's first feedback for her father's new day was to raise the teacup to her mouth, look at him from below, and then wink at him. Jan responded with a half-frowning face, declaring that he didn't share her charade. Then he thought of a way to announce the loss of his wolfness.

He exchanged glances with Vian, who shrugged her shoulders. Tara looked at her father again, this time disappointed. Dana looked at Tara while chewing his food from the corner of his mouth before commenting on the current peculiar case.

"I feel a calamity," he said, his words mixed with chewing; a voice Jan always hated when he heard it from him. "Has any of our relatives died?"

"Since when do you consider the death of a relative or even ten of them a calamity?" asked Jan. "Even if I die, you'll stand by my corpse and shrug your shoulders and tell me, 'This how life is, dude. In the end, we will all die.'"

"Okay, I'll rephrase my question," Dana said. "What calamity has befallen you all?"

"You were the first calamity befell us fifteen years ago and is still in effect," Jan said as he lifted a sandwich of bread and eggs to his mouth. "Then why did your mind go to calamity?" his jaws moved as they chewed the sandwich. "Why isn't it a grace that descended upon us? For example, we won... we won..."

He stopped.

"Won what?" Dana asked. "A million-dollar lottery?"

"We won…"

"A two-million-dollar lottery?"

Jan was inattentive to his son's inquiries as the word "grace" was ringing in his head insistently. His jaws were moving quickly one over the other, grinding the sandwich in a way that made Tara happy. She imagined him as a sheep chewing the cud.

Suddenly, Jan's eyes lit up with a ray of triumph. A broad smile appeared on his face. He swallowed hard, wiped his hands up and down on his ribs, and then beat them together once so hard it made the three of them wince. Then he laughed louder than he had ever heard himself laugh before.

"Oh God, how abundant are Your blessings!" he shouted with joy. "Yes, yes, it's a great blessing that has come down upon us. We are back to the happy family as before."

Vian guessed his next words. Jan raised his hands to chest level as if preparing to pray.

"I'm pleased to announce to you on this day, which, although it doesn't coincide with any religious or national occasion, is a glorious day. It's your deliverance from a nightmare that befell you in the previous period," he said with enthusiasm that surprised him that it was real. "My accursed wolfness has plunged this house into chaos and a perpetual state of war. The effect of the accursed wolf's venom has gone away from my blood forever. And now,

I've returned to my nice human nature that all people love, including Milo, the dirt… the handsome dog."

While the three didn't seem affected by the news, Jan was mocking his excessive enthusiasm.

I don't know when to get rid of this innate idiocy? he thought to himself. *When a simple truth comes to me on its feet, I need time to discover it. How did I not think of this solution? I'm Tara's stupid sheep par excellence.*

Then he said to them, "It seems that joy has tied your tongues. I understand it's a celebratory shock, as psychologists say. When I say psychologists, I don't mean female social researchers who nervously tap their notebook with the tip of their pen."

Jan forced himself to stop his announcement before losing control of himself and saying what would expose his false motives.

Dana pursed his lips and moved them to the side of his mouth, showing his disinterest in the matter.

"I don't think it's a big gain," he said. "Nothing will change in this house. You weren't hitting or biting us. You were just snarling and that's all. We became used to it as we were used to the growling of the dog.. oh, well, the lions in Tara's favorite animal TV channel. It wasn't nice of you to hurt the walls and doors of the house with your head before that wolfy situation."

The comment frustrated Jan before Tara intervened to oppose her brother.

"No, it's very, very good," she said with enthusiasm that Jan didn't miss its fake nature. "We felt like we were living with a wolf that might eat us."

"You say this because the non-wolfism is in your favor," Dana said.

"The what?" Tara asked.

"When you grow up, you'll understand the expressions of adults," he replied. "Until then, I'll make my words clear to you: it's in your best interest that your father is no more a wolf."

Of course, it's in her best interest, that exploiter, Jan said to himself. *But she'll regret it when she finds out that she can no longer blackmail me. As for you, teenager, I promise you a record blow as a penalty for your hyper-record insolence. A twelve-inch diameter reinforced concrete pile into each of your mucus-filled nostrils.*

Jan felt like he had become alone as before. He thought of what to do next. Vian's hand, which he felt on his arm, awakened him from his worry.

"Whether you're a wolf or not, we all love you," she said.

Dana looked at his plate and fiddled with the spoon on it.

"But that wasn't what you said before," he said to his mother. "At least before we go to see the misogynistic officer."

Jan turned to him.

"And what did she say?" he asked.

"I don't remember exactly, but it was all flirting with the wolf man and no other," Dana answered. "I just remember her saying something resembled a violent romantic movie dialogue: either Jan or nobody."

Jan turned back to his wife and looked at her with eyes full of gratitude, then took her hands in his.

"How great you are, my Vivi," he told her. "You adored me when I was a wolf. And when I lost my great... I mean, my damned wolfness, I didn't degrade in your eyes."

"You're my husband," she said. "Spouses should accept each other despite all their shortcomings. You accepted me despite my behavior that you didn't like."

"Thank you, thank you, my 'either Vivi or nobody'," Jan said and then let go of Vian's hands. "And I'm sorry."

"For what?"

"For holding your hands with mine, stained with boiled egg fat," he replied. "As you know, I smear my hands while eating, even if it is dry bread, just as a sheep stains its mouth with grass."

Dana got up. "We'd better leave you two alone," he said, turning then to Tara. "You too, get up. Disgusting things allowed only for over eighteen are going to happen here."

Tara got up from her chair. "When you wash your hands, Dad, come to my room to play with me."

"Your father won't come," Vian said. "He'll play with you when he wants and the way he wants."

In their room, Jan asked Vian, "Were you serious when you said that couples should accept each other even if their hands were stained with boiled egg fat?"

"Yes, even if they are stained with animal fat of cooked head and trotters."

"This's new to me," Jan said.

"And to me," Vian said.

"Now I understand why you don't like feminist activists who interfere in the family matters of society," he said.

"It was an instinct in me," she said. "And I understood it now."

Jan looked around the room.

"Don't you think this place doesn't fit Platonic romance?"

"Although this's my first time to hear this term, I understand what you mean and I agree with you," she said. "How if we go back to the airport fence at exactly twelve o'clock at night and watch the moon on its fourteenth night, which will be tonight, as it rises from behind the eastern mountains on our new life?"

"Wow," Jan said. "It's better than the suggestion I had in mind."

"Which was?"

"To watch the moon from the roof of our house while eating popcorn as if we were watching a movie."

Less than an hour before midnight, Vian instructed Dana to take care of his sister until they would return.

While riding in their car, Jan saw the full moon close to the middle of the sky.

"I trust your astronomical information, honey, when you said that the moon rises over the mountains at midnight," he said. "So surely, something happened to the universe and caused the moon to hasten to ascend in the dome of the sky. Maybe it rejoiced at our new life."

"This was in a story I wrote in language class when I was a child," she said. "It was a story full of fiction and incorrect scientific information."

"Since you wrote it, those things were real and scientific in ancient times," Jan said enthusiastically. "But then the world went awry and the moon began to change its habits."

Vian drove to the airport. None spoke, but they were smiling. They reached the airport fence where they had come the previous two times.

Jan asked her, "Should we light a fire as we did before?"

"We don't want to reveal our whereabouts," she answered. "Besides, the light of fire will drown out the moonlight."

Jan and Vian sat next to each other, crossing their hands around their knees. They remained silent, and then lay on their backs, looking at the moon. They heard a distant howling.

"Wolves or dogs?" asked Jan.

"It doesn't matter," Vian replied, "We don't need either."

"Yes, and even if the pack came and offered me a bite that is guaranteed to have an effect, I wouldn't accept it," he said.

"Yes, we don't want anything from them," Vian said. "We're human beings and we'll fight to remain human beings."

Jan noticed a small, dark arc of the full moon. "Who is this hungry creature who bit off a piece of the moon?" he asked.

"It's a lunar eclipse," Vian replied. "If we had followed the news, we would've known about it."

"I'm afraid that this insatiable creature will continue to devour the whole moon and ruin our Platonic night," Jan said.

"Look on the bright side, my dear."

"This's the bright side of the moon that we now see turning as dark as the other side."

"I mean, look on the bright side of this eclipse and of everything in life," she said.

"Uh, I get it. Something like: the eclipse will be complete and the world will darken and our night will be more romantic."

"Exactly."

"And the moon allows his wife, the earth, to deprive the people of his presence and keep him for herself for a certain period."

"Yes, yes."

"And if it's a partial eclipse, they'll appear together as if they're embracing."

"Yes, three times."

"And if it's a bloody eclipse, it's because the moon has sacrificed himself for his wife, the earth."

"Oh, my dear, how romantic you are. If all spouses were like this, divorces wouldn't happen."

"Did you know that during my time of foolishness and beating my head because of your behavior, I never thought of divorcing you? I was clinging to you like a hungry mouse clinging to a piece of cheese."

"Really?"

"Of course. Have you ever heard me say a word that indicated I wanted to leave you?"

"No. Keep going."

"In what? Proofs of my attachment to you?"

"No. In your romantic analogies."

"Okay, take this. God created a man and a woman," he said.

"He said to the woman, 'Your husband is your world,'" she said, leaning her head toward his shoulder.

"He said to the man, 'Treat the woman with kindness, for she is as delicate as a glass bottle. Don't break her,'" he said, wrapping his arm around her head.

"And he said to the two, 'I have created love and mercy between you," she said.

"If the universe were in the hands of war enthusiasts," he said, "they would say, 'We have created conflict and competition between you, and whoever fails to do so will be crushed.'"

"If it were in the hands of the worshippers of lusts, they would say, 'family isn't necessary. Pleasure is everything,'" she said.

"Then love and compassion would disappear and carnal desires would prevail," he said.

"But God created a man and a woman holding hands to build a bearable world," she said.

"And after they die, they will come back to life and hold hands toward a world of eternal happiness," he said.

Part of the moon darkened, leaving a black crescent facing west. The crescent continued until it covered the entire moon. The moon remained dark, then a luminous crescent moon appeared, heading east.

"Look," Jan told his wife. "Once like this, and once like that. This is complementarity in life. One thing complements the other."

"As you complete my missing pieces and I complete yours."

"So, a part of my soul becomes in you and a part of your soul becomes in me."

"Do you remember the last thing you said?" Vian asked.

"Yes, and I'm not surprised that I remember it," he replied. "The man and the woman will hold each other's hands to enter into a happy world without death."

"Are we going to live together in that world, Jan?"

"Yes, together and forever."